The Secret Alchemist

Caroline A Connell

First published in 2013 as “From Gold To Iron.” This edition published in 2013.

ISBN: 1484881915
ISBN-13: 978-1484881910

First published in 2013.

The Secret Alchemist

To my husband and daughter,
for your unending
love, support and belief

Prologue

Sweat poured off Hectors' unkempt hair. His hands shook on the wheel.

"I was just taking this guy to the restaurant at the end of the block. Can't have been doin' more than thirty."

But the officer was having none of it.

"Get out of the vehicle and spread 'em."

He hadn't seen the kid. Honest. Just sprang out of nowhere. Not his fault, no way.

But the kid's mother was wailing to high heaven, louder than the ambulance responding to the cop's 11-41, and Hector knew, without looking, that the kid was already dead. The way his body had rolled up and over the hood. The crunch of soft bone against yellow metal. The eyes that widened and bulged in fear before the face smashed into a red and pulpy mess on the windscreen.

It's not my fault, he wanted to scream.

He watched his fare climb out of the back of his cab and start to give a witness statement to the cop's partner. He checked out the suit, the cufflinks, the tie, and the shoes. He noted the watch discreetly tucked under a crisp, white shirt cuff.

Six months ago that was me, Hector thinks. Yeah, six month ago I was just like you. No time between appointments. Presentations to investors. Dinner with clients.

But not now. Not since his whole world came crashing down last year. Not since he lost his job as an analyst. Not since global financial markets collapsed and banks and financial services firms shed employees and in some cases collapsed utterly, a mere ghost of a memory barely months later.

I'm not a loser, he thought. I'm a decent guy pulling a double to make ends meet. I'm paying my way. No social for me and my family.

Can't you see, he wanted to yell; can't you see I'm a good citizen? I'm not a child murderer. I'm a father myself.

But the crowd gathering around him didn't see it that way.

"He kept rubbing his eyes, officer," he heard the (his!) passenger tell the traffic cops.

Rubbing his eyes? You'd be tired if you worked as hard as I do, he thought. But, as he sat in the back of the patrol car on his way to the station, the shock began to wear off. Reality, dumb, grinding, relentless reality set in.

He had killed a child. No matter how you looked at it, he had killed that child. And he'd killed a child when he was tired. Maybe if he hadn't been tired, he'd have seen the child. Been able to stop. Maybe not, too. But maybe, maybe, and enough of a maybe to tear into Hector's soul.

The financial markets, though, didn't see any of this. What they saw was the US$2.6 trillion put forward by the Federal Reserve. The £325bn provided by the Bank of England. The US$ 696bn handed out in Japan. The €1 trillion handed to beleaguered banks in Europe.

The financial markets saw all of this money and

reacted to chase short term gains, as was their habit. They didn't see Hector, for now. They didn't see little Denzel, who was playing tag with his mother and ran into the road and who was hit by Hector. No-one saw John, the bystander who hadn't been able to get an emergency dental appointment and was in so much pain after trying to pull a tooth himself. Denzel died in his mothers' arms as they didn't have medical cover. John collapsed with a heart attack, a victim of undiagnosed low blood pressure.

Hector didn't carry insurance and committed suicide before he could be tried with Denzel's death, crucifying himself with shame. No-one saw Denzel's mother dump his pet rabbit by the roadside, nor the truck driver who flattened it fifteen minutes later on his way to the extra delivery now included on his round for the same pay. No-one noticed John's parents saddled with debt from his unfinished college degree, and crippled by guilt from not carrying cover after their job terms and benefits were reduced. No-one witnessed Hector's wife lose her faith in God. No-one saw Hector's daughter smoke crack when she realized she now had no chance of going to college.

What financial markets saw was the absurdly vast sums of money handed to them by governments around the world. Money that could have built roads and schools. Money that could have trained armies of teachers and plumbers and nurses and software engineers. Instead of hard core investments in the people and infrastructure that make up a modern economy, financial markets got more cheap debt and were placated, their addiction satiated for now.

Chapter 1

"Stuff that for a game of soldiers."

It's a bleak day in February, and Arlene and I are dodging the rain in a steaming coffee house in downtown Budapest. Not the most glamorous of surroundings. Budapest may be a great tourist destination in the summer, when boats bob on the Danube, but we have wandered around, seen a few buildings, like you do, and are soaked – feet sodden inside business heels, rain breaching our showerproof business raincoats.

We are visiting Budapest on business, or rather we are staying at the airport hotel on business, which isn't quite the same. People think that international travel is glamorous, and sometimes it is, but a lot of the time you fly in and out of a place without going further than the airport hotel. And this is one of those times. If you haven't done it before, it can be hard to picture, but it goes something like this.

You catch your international flight on a Sunday, so that you can be 'on location' for the start of the business week. On arrival at the hotel, you and your colleagues check in before getting together in some beige and grey meeting room to run through what lies ahead. You eat in the hotel restaurant, ambience best described as air-conditioned funeral parlour. There's usually piped musak, 'though if you're really unlucky you are treated to bar noise drifting up through a vast atrium, which is open to all floors, all thirty of them. Which means that if you are truly unlucky it filters into your room, so you can never quite get away from it, and it keeps you awake until the last bar hog hits the sack.

But this time you've checked out the hotel on the web before booking it, and bagged yourself a quiet room, so after eating you part from your colleagues and go explore the hotel. There's usually a gym. It's a small room, grey walls, with maybe a couple of treadmills and a bench press. Run on one treadmill and you brush arms with the person on the other. There's no music or TV, and no staff. You need to use your key to get in. You contemplate, briefly, what would happen if you were in there, in your lycra, thumping along on the treadmill and a nutter were to let himself in. You realise that you would have zero chance of escape. No one would hear or see what happened as the gym is tucked away at the end of a corridor in a dark nook of the hotel. And it smells, faintly, but persistently. You decide you'll go for a run in the morning instead.

Alternatively, you explore the hotel and discover that the gym faces onto the bar. Oh lovely, now you can sweat away whilst saddo sales executives watch on. Even worse, the swimming pool faces the bar too, so you can wobble around in your swim costume and really get the guys going. Hey, dignity, who needs it? All in all, it's not an attractive prospect, and you decide to go for a run in the morning instead. You make a mental note to pick up a map in the lobby.

By now it is 7.30pm local time. You are six time zones behind home, so actually it is 1.30am and all you really want to do is go to bed. You wander back into the lobby, to pick up a map. They're on sale in the shop.

The hotel lobby shop is a unique institution. It sells things you need (toothbrush, paracetamol) and things you know you never will. Cards for occasions you didn't know existed (cherish your golf partner, anyone?), fridge magnets (city skyline, football, friendship), magazines (friendship, golf, sex).

Themes start to emerge, and for all the pizazz of the hotel you find yourself in the cultural wasteland of comfort eating and comfort shopping, where emotion is downloaded to cards and never spoken. In amongst the heartbreak you find the two things you are looking for, a local map for the morning, and a postcard to make your gran's day back home. You negotiate with the attendant for a postage stamp, and retire to your room to write your card.

The last thing you do before you go to sleep is check your email and send a couple back to the office. They will arrive marked time back home, so 2.30am. You'll look macho and dedicated and on top of your game.

You wake at 3am, and can't get back to sleep. Your body thinks it is 9am. You give up, get up and switch on your email. You discover that the lawyer you travelled with sent out an email even later than you. And it was complicated, a review-of-agreement sort of thing. What you don't know is that he wrote it before he left home and only sent it once on location, so he could look macho and dedicated and on top of his game.

You read the agreement and send back your comments. It's 5.30am and you need a coffee so you wander down to the lobby, where large, stainless-steel coffee urns (made in Malaysia) sit, steaming. You fill your Styrofoam cup and retreat to your room. You kill a few more minutes drinking coffee and watching the weather channel with the volume turned down low, then you put on your lycra and head out for a run.

If you are truly lucky, you can run from your hotel past some wonderful sight, such as the White House in Washington DC, or down the Champs Elysee in Paris, when the city is waking up to a new day and you can savour that early morning moment of silence, freshness and anticipation that only those hours bring: you feel you have been part of the city in some small way, even if you haven't lived it. More usually, you step over bums and winos, running along windy and soulless streets, past office blocks and car parks (where you run that bit faster) and discount stores.

You have probably breathed in heaven knows what in lead and ozone before you get back to the hotel, but you feel good and righteous and after your shower you head off to your 7am breakfast meeting feeling sleek and shiny and confident.

Alternatively, you fall asleep again at around 6.30am, miss your breakfast meeting and only just make it into the lobby to catch a taxi with your colleagues.

Not good.

Chapter 2

So here we are in glamorous Budapest. We are part of a team of ten people negotiating a five billion dollar merger. There's the lead negotiator, Brett Sinclair: early fifties, oddly even-coloured dark hair (dyed?), and set in his ways a little, sometimes wearing a vest under his shirt, sometimes wearing a jumper under his suit jacket, like guys all over the world filling commuter trains and buses. His business travel wardrobe looks to have been honed by years of international travel, with specialist chino-esque trousers that barely crease, a sleeveless chino jacket with oodles of useful pockets that make him look part tour guide, part big-game hunter, and a roll-along suitcase with a zip-off laptop holder with the correct logo.

There is Evan, a lawyer who specialises in approaches to competition authorities, and is ridiculously good at his job, plus another lawyer, Chip Cady, on secondment from our US subsidiary and handling legals for the entire transaction. There is also an endearingly affable Polish guy responsible for assessing the operational issues, for which read, check that the other guys' bits of machinery work and that they haven't polluted the environment so badly that you wouldn't touch their business with a barge pole. His full name is Jozef Tadaszczak, but he insists we call him Tad, and it has stuck.

We work for a large multi-national conglomerate, and the merger will involve all parts of a global business. We're headquartered in Switzerland but our biggest subsidiaries will be significantly impacted by this deal so are fielding experts in some areas. So, our finance team has a lead, Johann, who looks after the project globally and the overall position, but has to consult regularly with the Finance Directors of each of these subsidiaries. These guys can review, amend and indeed veto what Johann proposes, and if they don't like what he proposes they often call in the local CEO to argue their case. Johann is responsible for all of it, and all parts have a vested interest in coming up with proposals that will be acceptable across the piece, in all of the other affected countries as well as their own backyard. It's fair to say that Johann spends vast amounts of time negotiating and counter-proposing and producing the analysis necessary to support positions taken. He's like a one man United Nations and judicial authority, all rolled into one.

It's a complex way of doing things. Our counter-party is also a multi-national conglomerate, head quartered in Sydney, Australia, and with a reputation for no-nonsense leadership. They field just one person for each area. They look formidable, sorted, ahead of the curve. And very bemused by *our* team structure and process. They give every impression of thinking that they will be able to exploit this situation.

The plenary session, all ten of us and six of them, has quickly unfolded and we have moved into team sessions. The tax teams' sessions are a gem, and Arlene and I are up against Arthur. We have met before, lunch has been and gone today, and we are becoming used to one another.

We are arguing about the one perennial topic that vexes us, and has since the start, namely, what will be the structure for this merged business? Sounds complicated but it is a bit like asking yourself what sort of marriage you prefer.

At one end of the spectrum is what could be described as a more old-fashioned sort, where there is one person in control, usually the husband. He dictates where they go on holiday, what they spend their money on. His wife probably has an allowance, but in reality gets on with home life. She has no idea how much he earns, and where all the money goes. At the other end of the spectrum you have a marriage of equals. Whether or not the wife works they both regard one another as equal, all important decisions are made by the two of them, and their wealth is shared.

There are shades of marriage in between, but essentially that is what you are trying to decide.

Arthur opens with a wide-ranging salvo about the cost of what we proposed earlier in the day. He is throwing large sums of money in the air and Brett's pursed lips tell me that he is concerned. Is this true? Can our sensible proposal really be so costly?

Then Arlene asks a question. It's a simple one.

"Arthur, I'm just a lawyer, not a numbers guy: would you help me understand how your numbers are put together?"

She has a lovely southern USA accent, plays the belle real well with big brunette curls and a charming smile, but she is a tiger, and he just hasn't spotted this yet. As she takes us into what becomes a delightfully lawyerly cross-examination, it becomes clear that Arthur's numbers don't stack up. Pure blancmange, nonsense on stilts, based upon assumption and assertion, rather than fact. As we work together to carve away each element to his argument, the amount of money purported to be involved shrinks, as does the likelihood of the problem ever happening. A dead cert cost of two hundred million dollars disappears into thin air, and in a little over fifteen minutes. I make a mental note to myself: don‘t take a word Arthur says at face value. And another: she is *good.*

Arthurs' stock has plummeted, but strangely he doesn't look embarrassed. More likely, annoyed. But as this is an argument he thought he had won back in New York, maybe he has reason to.

We are trying hard not to smile. Our plan just got delivered.

The session breaks up.

Chapter 3

So, Arlene and I have found ourselves at a loose end. The teams will reconvene in their entirety in the evening, but we're all done. There are no agreements to produce, or read. I've updated our tax leads with a run-though of Arthurs' defeat (blow by blow, all very exciting, but it's kept serious and professional) and produced a joint note of meeting with Arlene. Email inboxes are dealt with, work is up to date, and this isn't the first time that we have found ourselves in this sort of position either. So, and for once, we boldly decide that we will venture away from the scene of the action and actually take a look around the city we are visiting.

Shock, horror! Actually venture away from the negotiating table? Correction, not 'negotiating', we aren't allowed to negotiate whilst on Hungarian soil: we are 'exchanging views' and 'seeking to understand one another's' position'. Whatever, a macho and dedicated and on top of their game player surely doesn't do this? This is not in the rule book. We, on the other hand, reason that we are in this position because we are so damned dedicated and capable, and we have to find *something* to do while we wait for the guys to catch up. Maybe.

So, we jump in a taxi, and head downtown, and

this is how we find ourselves, an hour and a half later, dodging the rain in a steaming coffee house.

We have wandered around the Castle and back across the Chain Bridge to Váci Street. Visiting tourist sites with someone you don't know is an exercise in overt politeness, but the great thing about visiting downtown Budapest is that Arlene and I have had time to talk and just get to know one another more, which I am hoping will stand us in good stead commercially throughout the rest of the deal (and why I am doing this).

We're an odd couple. I'm twenty-eight years old, tall, red-headed and very English and polite – everything is always 'interesting.' She's a forty-something brunette from New Orleans. I keep my wild hair under control with a short crop, she maintains fabulously big curls. She wears make-up, I have trouble finding my mascara and go for the natural look. I have no kids, she had her children early in her career and how has a pair of teenagers with hormones running at full tilt and exams in the offing.

In a lot of ways, we appear to be opposites, divided by our common language, yet here we are spending time in one another's company, and managing to increasingly agree with one another.

We have wandered doggedly around in the grey and the rain, sticking to headline tourist sights, but as time wears on I realize that, like me, she would have loved to have visited the museum based around the activities of the communist era secret police, but was too polite, in the taxi downtown, to mention it. And together we have ended up wet, totally soggy, and in need of warmth and resuscitation. We virtually dove into the coffee house, when we spotted it, and even the presence of other refugees from the rain, similarly sodden, didn't mar the experience. If anything, it lent an air of the warm, conversational atmosphere of the original, from centuries ago.

We catch a taxi back to the hotel having built a strong rapport, something, I suspect, she was as keen on as me.

Chapter 4

We first met back in January 2011. The Grand Poobah at our company had been in secret talks with the Grand Poobah from Arthurs' company the previous September, secluded in an extremely luxurious boutique hotel just outside Cannes. The result? They decided that they would like to merge each group's widget businesses. But the specifics weren't agreed, not even the prices involved. So teams were formed on each side. Team members relocated desks to some secret location so they could huddle together and keep things hush hush. They had lunch together. They couldn't even tell their boss. Well, they could, he'd be kind of worried otherwise. But no names, no numbers (not that there were any, anyway).

Confidentiality agreements were signed. The teams dreamt up special communication codes. We were to be known as 'Axis'. They would be 'Wildcat'. The deal would be known as 'Kingdom'. At one point there was tentative talk about Arthurs' team to being referred to as 'Assassin' but referring to someone as assassin probably isn't a good opening gambit if you want to set up constructive discussions, so it wasn't pursued. In every email, memo or agreement, these could be the only names used. The hunt was on and we all knew it.

After a couple of months of stage-setting a meeting was called: time for the tax teams from each side to meet up and talk tax. There was a small problem on our side: I am a specialist in tax law, but this was my first global merger. So, bottom line, I was relatively inexperienced.

"No worries," said my boss, Hans. "You're bright and a quick learner, Teddi, and your judgement is excellent. That's why we've chosen you for this: I'll help all that you need so you can learn as you go along."

I tried to research merger structures, get ahead of the curve pre the meet. My first port of call was Hans. Hans spent half an hour explaining the structure of a deal he negotiated a couple of years earlier. But, he wouldn't go into the basis for the tax planning used: he only seemed to know it in very generic terms and blustered through my requests for detail. And that was it. Not the most comprehensive outline of issues I could ever have hoped for it must be said. I made a metal note: is my boss all talk when it comes to coaching others? Does he know anything apart from that deal? And does that mean that, actually, I am on my own on this one?

I decided that I should spend a quality hour or two with one of the big hitting lawyers or accountants that advise in this area. There are a few in Geneva and the City of London that I could get with very quickly and easily, but Brett said no.

"No, Teddi, no can do. Too much risk of this spilling out, you know how these firms talk with their overseas offices. Next thing you know, their local partners would spill the beans with our subsidiaries around the globe and then where would we be? Industrial action, management blocks, you name it: complete uproar and a deal halted in its tracks before it gets going. No, Teddi, can't happen. Must stay absolutely quiet and confidential, what."

I can't help but think that the client confidentiality rules of the top firms would take care of that, but if I can't spend on fees, I can't spend on fees, no matter what the reason.

So here I am, sat on a plane on the way to New York. It's a Monday in early December. I have had zero support in preparation for the meet and have been researching academia. I am trying to read a couple of books I have found but they seem very basic. I am feeling way exposed and just cramming all I can. As if this isn't enough, in front of me a guy in a stetson has pushed his seat back to recline and is snoring loudly. I'm trying to think of angles but even in business class, with all its space, I can't hear myself think. And the sound is disgusting. Some people are ok when others snore but I can't stand it, and this is of the full-on, open-mouthed variety, whistling, snorting and gagging at top volume. I make a mental note: if anyone ever wanted to torture me they would just have to snore; I would 'fess up in minutes. Definitely my own Room 101.

This can't carry on so I lean forward, reach around the edge of his seat, and ever so gently prod his arm. I sit back in my seat, awaiting blessed release, but no dice, so I try again, this time less a prod, more a gentle shake. This is equally ineffective, he carries on snoring without even so much as the briefest of pauses. Oh heaven help us, I'm getting nowhere. After a press of the button a stewardess comes to my aid.

"I'm sorry to bother you, but the passenger in front is snoring rather loudly. Is there possibly anything that you can do to waken him, or somehow get him to sleep more quietly?"

She looks at me, with an air of sympathy and apology. It probably isn't the nicest of sounds for her, either.

She says "I'll see what I can do", but her expression tells of having tried this sort of thing before, and failing. Getting a snorer at full throttle to hear you is like farting against thunder: an exercise in futility and pointlessness.

She rests her hand on the back of his seat and leans in.

"Excuse me, sir." An expectant look. "Excuse me, sir".

But she gets nowhere, so I spend the best part of a seven hour flight with the headphones on, and I still can't drown out the torture. By the time we land at JFK I have achieved diddly squat and have the headache from hell.

Arlene has agreed to meet me at JFK and drives me to her office for a quick tour and a chat. She is being the most charming host to my visit, and we have dinner together at my hotel to start to get to know one another. She is super experienced in M&A work in general, and US issues in particular. I am almost asleep in the soup, but even in this befuddled state even I can see that she would be a real asset to the talks with Wildcat the next day.

"Look, Arlene, Brett's describing the talks with Wildcat tomorrow as preliminary, but you and I know they're important."

"Teddi, this is where the scene is set, where the shape for future negotiation is decided."

"Quite. Now the way I see it, you have been briefed about the existence of the deal by Brett so that you can provide expert input and review when needed. Just like our in-house experts from other countries."

Arlene follows my train of thought.

"So you're suggesting that I join tomorrow's talks?"

"Exactly. You have a wealth of experience in these issues, and the talks would of course benefit from that. But you know what? Whilst neither of us knows Arthur personally, by background we both know that he has spent large parts of his career outside Australia including the States, before ending up back in Sydney, so will be particularly up-to-speed on USA tax issues. Add to which, both Wildcat and Axis's widget business has skin in the game in the USA. I think we'd be foolish to enter the ring with him without having some weight in the bout too."

"Teddi, I hear what you say, and agree totally. I'll look to my diary and see if I can re-arrange my ten o'clock. Would that work?"

"Thanks, Arlene. If you could you ping me a quick email just to confirm, I'll let Arthur know. We're meeting at their lawyers offices but if you'd like to meet me just before, we could maybe plan what we could achieve from the meeting?"

I know my eagerness is on display. This is test of trust. Will she turn out to be the one person who will actually get on side and work with me to deliver this deal? I have no problem in giving credit where credit is due, and I have a strong feeling that she will be an invaluable asset to this team.

"Teddi, of course. There is a lot riding on this deal and it will be a pleasure to work with you on it. Now I can see you are just all in. I'll join you for breakfast, all things being equal, say 7am?"

And she wisely leaves me to get a good nights' sleep ready for the day ahead.

Chapter 5

The next day we meet Arthur for the first time. We're a small conclave of tax egg-heads, cloistered in a windowless room with coffee and donuts. From our side there's Arlene and I. From theirs', Arthur and an aide. It's a great meeting. We outline some of the basic pros and cons of the alternative structures open to us, the pros and cons of the marriages the two businesses could make, such as typical costs. Statements are by their nature generalised, there can be no specifics at this stage, but the meeting is cordial. We are tax nerds talking tax, and the exchange is open and friendly. Every so often Arthur takes care to double check that I agree with some statement he has made, before we note it up on flip charts. I have the feeling that he is trying to tiptoe around some issues.

We wrap up after about three hours and have lunch together. It is still cordial and friendly, and I head out back to the airport to catch the seven pm flight back to Geneva, brief Brett by 'phone, and fit in a spot of Christmas shopping - a delicate watch, a fabulous leather bag, and a mountain of memorabilia. Typical airport shopping, really.

To us, the meeting is worthwhile as far as it goes. The next stage is to run the numbers, and find out what the costs and benefits really are. We have to decide what sort of investor we want to be, how involved we want our local businesses to be in the widget business once merged, and of course checking with our people in each country to identify any local specifics that aren't as yet on the table. There are lots of issues, not just financial, and we know that they all have to be worked on so we can come up with a plan that can actually be implemented. We agree to meet again in two months.

Arlene and I don't know what Arthur thought about the meeting, but he paid for lunch so he must be happy. On the plane I sit next to an exec from a beverages business who has been touring California, Texas and New York drumming up business. We have a great laugh, and rather too much alcohol, sorting out the world, making sweeping generalisations along the way and generally celebrating our successes. Even though my mouth feels as rough as the bottom of a budgies' bird cage by the time we land at Geneva at 7am the next day, I'm feeling on top of the world: this mergers and acquisitions lark is a doddle.

Chapter 6

Brett invites me to lunch. It's probably the first time we have talked mono-a-mono for any length of time since the team was formed. We're in a dining room at our headquarters, with a view that encompasses both the lake and the Jet d'Eau. I haven't been in one of these rooms before, and deliberately arrived a fraction early so that I could soak in the view.

Geneva is a real delight, busy, charming, yet genteel. It's the home of the European Headquarters of the United Nations, and many of its global agencies, such as UNHCHR and The World Health Organisation. As a major global centre for diplomacy it has in turn attracted other global organisations like the International Committee of the Red Cross and the World Trade Organisation, and with its major position as a financial centre is the home for many global businesses and hedge funds. Despite the presence of so many expats and international types it somehow manages to retain the charm and reserve of a small town. The only drawback to this ludicrous affluence is that it is a ridiculously expensive place to live. Local twenty-and thirty-something professionals, Swiss residents all their lives, haven't a hope of getting onto the property ladder, unless their parents already have properties to share. I'm an expat with a generous rental allowance, so am relatively immune, but the prices are still an eye-opener, and it's best not to translate prices back to your home currency (you'd keel over in shock). With its benign climate and gentle charm, it does make for a very pleasant place to live. I'm lucky to be here, and loving every moment of my posting.

It's a delightful setting, and Brett is all smiles, oozing charm. Makes lots of knowing winks whilst we talk.

"I bet you know all sorts of tricks, Teddi. Stock conversions, deferred taxes, what? I'm sure you are just the gel for us." Wink.

I smile, and look him in the eye from under my lashes, and laugh politely, as you do when a married guy thirty years older than you leers at you and you wouldn't touch him with a barge pole.

"That's very kind of you, Brett, (heh heh), thank you". Self-deprecate, self-deprecate, whilst at the same time wondering how quickly you can politely part company, and how fast you can run in stilettos.

"Well, there are various things we can look at, but it's a bit like playing with a Rubik's Cube. We have to create a solution that pulls all the strands together, get all the colours lined up on each side. Works for the key countries, solves the key tax problems, and enables the management team to operate how it wants. You know, the usual issues. And as yet we have no idea of Wildcat's agenda. "

He seems mollified, still smiling, but the eyes are steady, watching me. I'm being appraised. I suspect that he isn't entirely comfortable with me on the team. I'm female and young, neither of which seems to find favour. He knows that I have experience of European mergers, but am new to the global stage, 'though rapidly getting up to speed and leveraging my knowledge from other deals. Plus, I have been pre-warned about Brett.

Before I joined the deal Hans had taken me to one side in early January. He knew that the Kingdom deal was about to land on my desk.

"Teddi, we're moving you into a pure M&A role."

I think I must've looked shocked. This is the dream role in our organisation, what I wanted, and he knew I did.

"There's a huge job coming up, and the team leader will be Brett Sinclair. He led the Swiss Franc bond issue we ran last year?"

"Yes, I've heard of him. By all accounts, very confident in his grasp of the issues as I recall, and negotiated great terms with the banks."

"That's it. Now, we think that Brett is going to dump you in it. The job is huge. It really needs a Director to handle it, but no-one is available from our team. It's coming to you because you're bright and can learn, but you're jumping in the deep end, make no mistake about it. You'll be exposed."

He looks at me. I am a team leader, which is a senior job grade for my age, but a Director is a step ahead, sort of for the late thirty-somethings. He's waiting to see how I react, to see if the full weight of what he has said sinks in. Silence seems the best option, and I look right back.

"Brett's a tough nut to crack. He had dealings with Sarah last year on the bond issue, and played some pretty nasty tricks. I had to step in quite frequently to defend her corner and keep him in check. He'll make your life quite difficult."

Again, the pause to look at me. I can't ignore the knot in my stomach - being told that you are about to be shafted, and how, isn't a heart-warming exercise. I don't respond, but clearly I don't control my body language.

"Don't worry, Teddi. The management team know what's about to happen. Brett is bound to take a swipe, maybe more than once, but we'll protect you. We just need you to pick yourself up and keep on going, no matter what. Come to us when you need to, and leave the rest to us, OK?"

I'd been ok with that, which was how I found myself lunching with Brett. He's looking at me still, but it's not like with Hans. Hans looks at you to check you understand, to reassure, it's part of his overall communication style, no need to play games. With Brett, it's the opposite. When he smiles, only the bottom half of his face moves, and I find myself studying this half-smile, and wondering how it is possible. His mouth shapes a smile perfectly, and a laugh emerges occasionally, but it quite literally stops part way up his cheeks, and his eyes remain as they were, steady and cold, even when he winks. It's like being lured to supper by a snake, and finding that you're the main course. I'm remembering the conversation with Hans, and light dawns. Brett is weighing me up, working out how to play me, and how far he can push.

What do you do in this situation? Talk rapidly using lots of sexy tax terms? Lace your conversation with 'synergies', 'strategies' and 'stock or asset'? Drop in the odd battle story? Talk in bullets? Throw some numbers in the air?

He needs a floor show, and but he isn't going to get it. Being played isn't part of my personal style, and I don't see why I should suddenly fall apart.

We recover the conversation, and part promising one another to 'do lunch' again soon sometime, but I'm not sure either of us believe that will happen.

The dichotomy in his behaviour is unnerving. That is probably his aim, but I'd expected that we'd be discussing the New York meeting, and exploring how he wants the wider issues, such as management style, played.

For such a large deal, Brett doesn't seem keen on having anyone willing to work the issues with me. I even had to pull in Arlene unilaterally. It can't make sense to field a relative newbie on such a big deal without back up, surely? Arlene, though, is a bright beacon of hope right now.

Chapter 7

Which is why we have a meeting in Budapest two months later. In between, Arlene and I have been working numbers and issues like crazy. We've built a huge Excel model that reflects how taxes work for the different marriage scenarios. We've waded through pages of tax rules, like the European Union's Mergers Directive. It's a great piece of legislation, but Governments across the European Union haven't implemented it into local law in the same way. Bits that are missing in the UK are present in the Netherlands and Spain. Spain is proving to be great; they just adopted it wholesale. Just a pity there is so little of the widget business in Spain. Germany and France on the other hand have adopted only certain parts, using the excuse of conflicts with existing local law or something. Romania is a whole different ball game. And so on. So, we have to figure out which bit is there, and which is missing, before we can figure out how to fit the pieces of the jigsaw together.

And of course all of this craziness is theoretical. There's nothing in the textbooks to explain just how the French, or Danish or South African tax inspector will actually regard some of these transactions. What extra steps they will require before they approve what you do. Which tax incentives they have introduced to make their country attractive to international business, and compete against their neighbours. I've started to wish countries just agreed with one another about how to treat things.

So, we've spent our time dreaming up ways for the groom and bride to get hitched across the globe. Looking at what Romania does, how long it could take in Brasil, what documentation they require in Greece, what options we have in Japan, in China, in Australia.

Arlene looked at the US marriage and got quite excited. We had long telephone calls where she explained the obscure intricacies of exchanges, partnerships and capital that tax lawyers get excited about and bore everyone else senseless. She took me through rules about loans, and stock options, and the 401k plans that employees use to plan for retirement. My head swam. It was a very steep dive into some of the most complex parts of the US tax code and I had to fight to stay afloat, let alone keep up with her strong front crawl, but it was good stuff and a way forward emerged. We agreed the next meeting with Arthur.

This time we are all flying to Budapest. Brett seems quite excited about having another meet, and before we know where we are everyone is joining in the fun fest; Brett and his counterpart Gus, Johann and his counterpart Ed, and so on. Sessions are arranged in parallel to cover all the major areas. We cloister ourselves at a hotel near the airport.

We kick off the tax session, but this time everyone is there. Arthur gets to open. He outlines the outcomes of our last meet, and then something odd happens.

"We've agreed that the cheapest solution is to create partnerships in each country. We can then each repatriate our cash out however we want."

Huh? I don't think so. Immediate knee jerks on the Axis side of the table. Brett remains calm, but his florid cheeks edge toward puce. I think, oh dear God, Brett, don't die on me right now

Arlene and I look at each other. It's my turn.

"We didn't actually do that, Arthur. In fact, we didn't come to any conclusion at all. We simply identified some pros and cons of various structural alternatives." Sharp glances in my direction. Arthur leans in, but I head to cut him off.

"I have copies of the minutes of the meeting here with me; we circulated them afterwards, if anyone wants to look at them?" Pause. "You remember these Arthur, we agreed them by email a couple of days later."

Still silence from everyone else, but Arthur is leaning in again. Time to spin this around.

"Brett, Arlene and I circulated these around the team a couple of days after the meeting, if you recall? Now you know how Arlene and I operate, the tax tail doesn't wag the business dog. To progress this the tax folks really need to get a feel for how you and Gus want this merged business to operate. How do you want it to manage its' affairs? How much involvement do you think this baby will want from its' parents, or from the Axis or Wildcat businesses in each country?"

Both he and Gus are looking at me steadily. Gus doesn't blink but quietly murmurs "Go on."

Ok, I have the floor. Time to take a deep breath and make the pitch of my life.

"Try and look at it like this. There are around ten countries involved. Let's say that each country is represented by a couple who want to get married. So, if each couple get married, then to make any decisions overall you would have to get the agreement of each married person. Try to imagine having ten married couples in a room whenever you want to make a decision. For example, you might want to spend money in one country on new equipment. In this analogy, you might say that the couple get a new kitchen. But the other couples would be annoyed, couldn't they have a new kitchen too. Maybe the in-laws might wade in with comments too, from time to time. You could come up with ways for the couples to mediate and agree, but bottom line it would be a nightmare, a great, big, squashy quagmire of non-agreement and eventual stalemate."

"At the other extreme, you have the multiple stepford wife scenario. One guy decides everything, a head honcho if you will, with all the individuals doing what they're told. From a business point of view, most people would probably plump for this option, after all doesn't it sound easy?"

I can see Arthur straining in his seat. I can't let him in; time to press home the advantage.

"But these are just examples, extremes at either end of a wide range of options. If you go for the multiple marriage option for sure you can use losses locally against profits, what we tax folks call local grouping, but how much is that worth, and will it ever compensate for a business that can't function? Indeed, what other tax benefits might have been forgone?"

"You have to look at all the alternatives. Arlene and I have come up with a way of looking at the world that we think manages both issues. What we would like to do now is move to taking you guys through a high level overview of that idea, give you some food for thought."

I stop. I've been sketching figures on a flipchart whilst I've been talking, getting ready for the main pitch. Tax talk has a way of reducing even the hardest-headed businessman to a glassy-eyed jelly, and I'm in danger of overdoing it. Arlene has been nodding encouragement, so maybe I haven't done too badly, but I feel like some gladiator in the Coliseum waiting for the Emperor to signal thumbs up or down. You know the feeling, there are probably butterflies in your stomach, but right now your brain barely knows where your stomach is, so who knows?

"So how much is at stake, Teddi?" Again, from Gus.

A killer question. We have bugger all "real" data from the coal face, it's just too early in the deal to swap information. As Brett says, asking all of the countries involved to start projecting income for one part of their business for the next five years just isn't feasible right now.

"Well, we have our figures, and I'm sure Arthur has his for Wildcat, but as everyone here knows, we haven't yet got to a position where legally we can exchange that kind of detail. I believe that Evan can update us on our approaches to the various global competition authorities, maybe suggest when we will be able to expose that kind of information, but bottom line, unless we want these negotiations to grind to a halt in the meantime we are going to have to come up with some form of protocol to enable us to move forward. That way, once we can exchange data it will hopefully be like fitting pieces of a jigsaw together. "

Arthur looks pissed, big time.

"Teddi, we already know what our options are, we discussed that in New York, and…"

"Arthur, with respect, did we talk about any planning ideas?" I move straight into a scoping of our ideas, keeping to the points, calmly, collectedly, and nailing each one in turn.

Light dawns. It may be gibberish to most folks, but, and to give Arthur credit, whilst he may be a manipulative turd he knows his tax. I've pressed some of the buttons that get a tax person really excited, and he's no exception.

Now it's Gus' turn to look hacked off. But it's not with me, or Arlene, or Brett, or anyone on our side. He's just watched his own guy wobble, and when he requests time out, no-one is surprised.

Chapter 8

“Teddi, I thought we were going to outline our idea for the structure and management going forward.” Brett looks hacked off that the meeting hasn’t progressed as he had expected.

We are having a team debrief in an adjacent room, while Wildcat have theirs.

“Brett, what seems pretty clear is that they already have a fairly set idea about how they want to structure the deal…”

“This business of multiple local marriages?”

“Yes, that’s it. My impression is that the idea has come from Arthur, and Gus is following Arthurs’ lead. “

“But he isn’t fully conversant yet with all of Arthur’s thinking. Doesn’t know ours. Probably is withholding judgement until he sees all the facts. In his shoes, wouldn‘t you do the same? “This from Arlene, bless her.

“That’s right. He’s seen enough to have doubts about the advice he has been receiving, but probably not enough yet to run with our line of thinking. “

“And don’t forget, Brett, that we’re still in the early stages of the deal. He won’t commit yet until he knows the size of the pie.” Arlene again.

“That’s just the way I read it back there in the meeting, Brett. The Wildcat team aren’t ready yet to talk about an alternative. They need to be ready to review all options facing this joint venture first, and if we plunge too far into the idea right now, we risk seeing it lost in these early stages. "

"Well then how the hell are we going to take this forward, Teddi? We're trying to get to Heads of Agreement with Wildcat, we need this deal. "

This much is true. There is massive over-supply in the widget business, and neither business has the economies of scale to survive on its own for much longer. As far as we can see this deal with Wildcat is probably our last chance to find a value-driven opportunity. Goes without saying that Wildcat have probably guessed that. So, we are trying to negotiate with a strong hand, yet not blow things. Never an easy task. Having said that, it is fair to say that if Wildcat's widget business was in a brilliant state, they wouldn't be talking to anyone about a merger, so at least we have some room for manoeuvre.

"Hear what you say, Brett. Given that we can't get to an absolute conclusion on anything before due diligence, we already know that the Heads agreement won't be binding, yes? And we have taken the initiative in producing the first draft, yes? So maybe we take the lead and outline our idea in that document, at an extremely high level? "

"What happens if they don't agree?"

Chip steps in. "We could square bracket it, Brett. We already know that there could be other contentious issues treated that way."

Chip has been sitting in the background so far, absorbing what has been said. Square bracketing is a bit of a nonsense, it means agree to disagree, that what is in square brackets isn't part of the agreement. But, on the basis that it is easier to defend what is already there than try for wholesale removal, it makes a kind of sense to have your version in the official document.

Chip is one of those lawyers who is very, very good at producing what his client tells him. I've often been quite envious of a lawyer who is able to work like this. If their client, which is what Brett effectively is, tells them to paint a hoop pink with yellow dots and jump through it, they will, as long as it isn't illegal. Clients like Brett find this wonderful.

Tax folks in our business, on the other hand, are tasked to actively consider what will be in the interests of all parties in the deal. The local companies, the ultimate shareholders, the works, and spend much effort trying to get buy-in from multiple stakeholders. Sometimes it's just impossible – a quoted multinational group could have shareholders in the USA, in Europe, in Asia, in Latin America. Shareholders could be pension funds or individuals. On a lot of levels, the shareholders could have such widely varied requirements that meeting all of them is just impossible.

For example, you are sat on your sofa wondering what to do with your shares in that "tiger economy" company that you bought a few years back. It's done pretty well, there's a small profit. You took a bath on your technology stocks a few years ago. You'd like to sell up, start to reconstruct your battered portfolio. Trouble is, you've spoken to a broker and he has some worrying news. When you sell, the tax authority in that country will want you to pay some tax on the profit. You already know that you'll have to pay tax in your own country too. It seems a bit unfair, being taxed twice. Luckily for you, your best friend from college went on to become a tax lawyer, and he says it needn't be that bad. Some governments have realised that this situation is a bit unfair, and have agreed a set of rules between them to determine who gets a bite of the apple. Others don't have agreements with other countries, but do have their own rules to limit how they can tax. You're relieved, to say the least; with a bit of research you may well be home and dry.

At least that way is straight forward. Let's say you own those shares, and along comes some huge conglomerate, wants to take over the company. Trouble is, they don't want to pay you cash, they want to give you shares in the new super-duper merged company. As it turns out, you're actually quite happy with that. It will be a way to diversify your portfolio. But that broker is being a pain again.

"Sorry, old chum. They still want tax. Just because you haven't received cash, doesn't mean you haven't made a sale of sorts. "

Now that is grim; paying cash out when you've had no cash in is no-ones' idea of a good time, but over a beer one evening your friend allays your fears. You discover that some governments appreciate your predicament, and will allow you to defer the tax until you eventually sell the new shares. If you hold the shares for long enough you may even get a complete breather. Even if you don't, for every year you get a delay you are effectively being loaned money by the government, and they aren't charging interest. It's pretty much the cheapest finance you can find.

So what you learn, is that you need to find out the circumstances in which each of the tax authorities will tax you, and when they won't. You need come up with various ways forward.

You need work out how much each will cost you, or benefit you. Then you decide what to do.

It isn't just about technicalities, either. There is a strong moral aspect flowing through tax work. If the answer is really obvious, if a Government has put in place a tax break for businesses to use, then great, use the legislation. It's much like state aid, or benefits to the unemployed, or green cards that let you stay and work in a country. They're designed to help, but no Government wants them abused. Sometimes, tax legislation is hard to understand, even for tax bods. Sometimes it doesn't do what the Government said it would do. Sometimes it reneges on earlier promises, or agreements with other countries. Sometimes the same set of facts produce quite radically different outcomes in different countries. Countries do compete about tax – there is no one, homogenous rule telling a business what to do. Life would be so much easier commercially if countries adopted the same tax rules, but they don't, and in these situations, the Board of our business wants to form a view as to which way to jump. Boards take whichever view they deem most appropriate – that's their job. They review all pros and cons of options. The humble tax bod in our organisation tries to ensure that a sense of judgement, is applied to ideas, and that there is as much empirical, fact-based evidence to support positions taken as possible. External experts are frequently brought in for this purpose, particularly as no one person could feasibly know all rules, everywhere.

The Board also wonders about the reputation of the business: what, for example, if the idea were to get onto the front page of a national newspaper, would the company feel embarrassed, would it damage the company's reputation? The Board likes to know this sort of thing. It helps them decide a way forward when the route isn't clear cut.

So this is what a tax person does all day. Sometimes the answers are cut and dried, but usually it isn't so straight forward, and you have to ensure that intellect and judgement are applied in equal measure to understand just what you are dealing with. Getting a tax deduction for your charitable contributions can seem very straight forward, but ideas to evade taxes inhabit the deepest and murkiest end of the spectrum of possibilities, and in our organisation we like to steer well clear of these options as a matter of policy.

So, your average tax person spends a lot of time helping the business guys understand just where in the range the outcome lies. And Chip, being super smart, has fast realised that the tax issues on this deal aren't going to be resolved overnight so, hey presto, the square bracket solution.

"Let me get this straight. We go back into the meeting, we put our proposal forward, and we deal with any counter proposals and problems they raise, and they will. Our goal today is to ensure that our proposal is in the Agreement we sign. If needed, we concede square bracketing. Is this our plan?"

Arlene, Chip and I nod agreement. "That's right Brett".

"Right, plan agreed. Let's get back in there."

Which is why, later that day, and after another heavy session, Arlene and I find ourselves in a coffee house in downtown Budapest. And a month later, in March, we are back in Switzerland, reviewing the final draft of the Agreement. Which is signed three days later, and which has all the tax stuff square bracketed, but it's our strategy that is in there.

Chapter 9

"Well *that* was a depressing place to visit."

"I know, blight-blasted roads of empty retail space, neon-lit sex shops and battered sports bars…."

"I meant the plant, 'though that too."

Tad is pouring coffee.

"I mean, I've never seen a place that has so obviously been cutting out maintenance. It'll cost major dollars to get it up to the standard we've pledged to our investors. "

"Are things really that bad?"

Tad is our expert on operating matters, such as machinery maintenance, control of environmentally damaging materials and building use optimization. He's an absolute guru at running lean operations, that's why he was drafted onto the team in the first place, so it's got to be an issue if he notices it.

It's now late November and we're in an unused office on an industrial site on the outskirts of Philadelphia. Actually, we're not. We're in a meeting room in a city centre hotel that we are using as a base to debrief and plan our work, and are talking about the day we just spent in an unused office on an industrial site on the outskirts of Philadelphia. After Budapest we have moved onto running our own numbers and checking one another's: Wildcat's industrial plant in Philly is one of many that they own, and they're using it as a base for due diligence. Which is a complicated way of saying that we're digging through all of the data that they have disclosed, to see if there is anything in there that we should know about.

When you're looking to sell or buy a business, or go into a joint venture, there is a bit of a cat and mouse process where you each try to check whether there are any 'unexploded bombs' in the others' business performance. It might be waste spillage into the local ground water, or maybe perks for senior staff that you don't think are sustainable. It might be debts that you didn't realize they had, or even customers that are walking away. Maybe they're heading into a cash black hole. Could even be lousy industrial relations. All sorts of things really. At the same time, you're also looking for opportunities where you could improve performance, too. It might be you could introduce the really efficient machine operation that *your* factory floor teams have developed, or maybe you have a great process to mine customer data to optimize selling prices. Whichever, parties just want to be aware, so that they can take informed decisions, even walk away if they have to.

The moral question kicks in here, too. At this stage of a deal, there is no binding commitment to proceed, but commercially sensitive data may start to be reviewed by a competitor. In start-ups, there are nightmare scenarios of potential buyers using the process to, effectively, acquire knowledge, leaving the start-up stranded high and dry. So, you try to ensure that you disclose at the best possible stage you can, when there is more comfort. You ensure that your intellectual property is fully defended. You sign agreements that protect your intellectual property; after all, if the deal collapses and your competitor suddenly introduces a new technique in producing widgets (that you had patented the year before) then at least you have some form of legal redress (even if it will take a court case to deliver).

Tad has been spending months inspecting sites around the world, both ours and theirs, and has spent most of the time in Philly out on the manufacturing floor itself.

"Well, put it like this, the place has clearly been run on a shoe-string for a very long time. Absolutely the bare minimum of maintenance and investment. The machinery is heavily exploited. The buildings and machinery will need substantial investment over the next two to three years to replace and generally make fit for the next twenty years. And there is evidence of storage tanks recently having been moved."

"What does that mean?"

"Not necessarily anything. Alternatively, and if you wanted to be really paranoid, you'd think that they are distracting attention from ground spillages."

"So what will you do about that, Tad?" This from Brett, who has just walked through the door.

"Only one thing we can do, Brett." No pause from Tad, he is so very good at his job he takes this in his stride. "We run ground contamination tests, and let those speak for themselves."

"Ah, but what about our sites, Tad? Won't Wildcat want to run the same tests? Dare we let them?"

"Well Brett, I know these sites, and I feel reasonably comfortable with what they would find. I 'd be more concerned with setting the terms of the testing process, otherwise this will just turn into some playground slanging match."

"Ah, then I need to talk with Wildcat to set those terms, don't we? Leave it to me Tad" and Brett walks smoothly to the front of the room.

But Tad isn't finished.

"Actually, Brett, I've given that exact issue careful thought. We need to set parameters that give each side a reasonable opportunity to discover issues, yet not wrangle incessantly over trivialities. My counterpart at Wildcat thinks the same, and we have some ideas about the testing that we think would facilitate this."

Brett looks momentarily taken aback.

"We dropped an email about an hour ago to you and Gus. Maybe once you've taken a look we could discuss with them? They've already said they would be keen."

Brett now looks furious. His face is puce, and his nose strangely mottled and veiny. For a moment he doesn't reply, and we all stare, taken aback by the situation. Is he going to need CPR?

He recovers fast, and agrees to the call, but across the table from me I can see Arlene looking as perplexed as I feel.

What is going on?

Chapter 10

We've finished at the site in Philly, and are heading home. I'd travelled to Philly with Arlene, flying into Newark for a pre-meet with her, and both of us taking the train down. Over dinner one evening at our hotel, we realized that Arlene, Tad and I would be heading back to New York at the same time, Arlene to go home and Tad and I to catch flights back to Europe.

"Teddi, Tad, why don't you join my family and I for supper on your last evening, before you fly back?"

We knew Arlene lived in New Jersey on an hour's commute into Manhattan.

"At your home?" In the States it is a real honour to be invited into a colleagues' home, a sign of willingness to trust and form a strong working relationship. We were being invited in and I was impressed, and a little awed too.

"It would be my pleasure, Teddi, and my family would be delighted to meet you both."

"Well I'd be very happy to meet them, Arlene, so yes, please."

"Thank you, Arlene, that would be a pleasure."

And before we knew it, it was all agreed and planned. We'd head out from Philly at the end of the final day together, Tad and I would check into our airport hotel, then head to Arlene's. So, two days later, we found ourselves in a taxi heading out to Morristown on the I-78.

I'd seen the Garden State before, or rather I'd flown over it, coming in to land at Newark Liberty International Airport on an internal flight from Denver just a few days earlier. It had been Christoph's idea to fly out to Denver and try and get some early-season skiing in Vail before my trip to Philly. Although the season in Switzerland doesn't officially start until December, it is quite common, depending on the weather, to fit in a weekend here and there before then and we were hoping that the Rockies resorts would be open early, too. Christoph had been to Vail with his college buddies from MIT, but I hadn't been before, never even skied in the US, so this was going to be a first on many levels.

Christoph and I had met back in January. I'd been in Geneva since the summer before and spent most of my time hosting weekend visitors from back home, and heading back for friends' weddings and the like. But I'd begun to feel a little lost, like I was treading water, when Maertje appeared in an office down the hall from me one Monday. Another expat, we became friends and one day she invited me to a reception at one of the embassies in town to celebrate inter-governmental technological co-operation. Em needed someone to go the reception with, and I needed to develop my social life, so I had accepted, gratefully. Christoph had been there, part of a group of scientists invited along to address the assembled crowd about progress in particle physics.

He stood out - tall, dark-haired, with the sort of slightly craggy good looks that a man ages into. Our eyes had briefly met during the presentations, and I'd tried to think nothing more about it, when he suddenly appeared in front of me.

"Could I introduce myself? Christoph Dettwiler, Accelerator Physicist. I hope you didn't find our presentation too dull?"

"Teddi Wood". We shook hands, he held mine a little longer than I was used to. "Actually it wasn't boring, probably too brief for my tastes. I'm fascinated by the achievements in finding the Higgs Bosun particle, for example, but I must confess to wondering where we will end up with ideas like quantum entanglement and action at a distance. The possibilities are quite exciting."

He had looked momentarily startled.

"You are in the field too? Where? What are you studying? Have I heard of your research? "

I laughed. "Sorry to disappoint, but I'm not in the trade. I read Physics to A level in the UK. Pre-college? I love quantum physics, it makes sense to me whereas Newtonian laws just seem inadequate. I try to keep track of what is happening with background reading here and there, but the maths just blows my mind."

Oh my word. I had just revealed my inner nerd to the most handsome guy in the room. Disaster. Time to shut up. Strange thing was, he was smiling.

"Teddi, please excuse me, I can see our project head calling for my presence. Perhaps, we could meet for lunch sometime? Discuss our mutual interest?"

"Well, let's see what we can arrange," I had replied, sounding far more cool, calm and collected than I felt.

"May I have your number?"

I had passed him my card, with a smile.

"Thank you Teddi. Until then." And with that he was gone, into the throng, and I was more than a little stunned. I'd just been asked out!

Christoph had called the very next day. I was pleased - clearly he was very keen, and it was a relief to know that the request for my number wasn't just an excuse to get away. I had played it cool, and arranged lunch for a couple of weeks hence. From that point on, things had just evolved. By the summer we were in love (and I'd discovered that the head of project thing had indeed been an excuse, but one to hide how keen he felt and be able to ask me out over the phone rather than face to face, in case I blew him out). The trip to Vail was quite clearly a test of our relationship - our first major holiday together.

We had been fairly lucky with the snow. Conditions were probably nowhere near as good as they would be in, say, February, but it had been great fun to ski the huge mountains of the Rockies, rather than the short, sharp and neat Alps. Best of all, the trip had been a dream for the two of us. Christoph guided us around the runs, and somehow knew where to be at just the right time. We drank chocolate and watched the sun set over the bowls. We ate sushi and trout, dined casual and fine, at the bottom of the mountain and at the top. We relaxed on our balcony, wrapped in rugs, looking at the moon, talking about dreams, hopes and wishes, childhoods and college years, and laughed at one another's rotten jokes.

Once or twice we tested one another's views on life issues. I would never live with someone before marriage. Christoph wanted two children (at least!) A marriage was a partnership of equals, there for one another in good times and bad. We couldn't work out how a twin career marriage worked with children without employing half the world as nannies and cleaners (which was a slightly uncomfortable discussion to have, I had thought: were we negotiating something here?) And, despite high factor sunscreen, I managed to get sunburn, which was neither healthy nor a good look against my red hair. Christoph developed a ski tan, a reverse panda.

We'd flown back out of Denver late morning on the Friday, Christoph to connect at Frankfurt for Geneva, and me to fly internal to Newark Liberty (both dodging a change at Chicago O'Hare, which we'd decided we weren't going to attempt to transit).

Chapter 11

The flight across America had been a real eye opener: the view truly astonishing. As we lifted up from Denver, we immediately headed across the brownest vastness that I had ever seen. Creeks and canyons etched in brown, waterless and treeless. Crops irrigated in grungy circles. Fields bisected at large distances by empty roads. Occasional homesteads. After the Rockies, and from so far above, it looked so alien. I sat opened mouthed, watching it slide by. Gradually, the creeks acquired the occasional shrub or tree, and shade trees appeared by the homesteads. The green cover started to extend, to bends in creeks, then stretches, until the entire route would be marked in the landscape, a green ribbon against the brown. Terraces started to appear on the hillsides, and with it green fields, copses of trees and villages and towns. Suddenly the ground was green, lush and oozing fertility. Urban development appeared.

What was this and what had I just seen? The legacy of the dust bowl? Or just winter drabness in the bread basket of America?

And where were we now? Below us a powerful river spews its brown silt into a vast tract of water, port jetties barely occupied. It hit me like a sledgehammer – this must be the Great Lakes. Wow. Was this Duluth and we were skimming the bottom edge of Lake Superior? Or maybe we were as far south as Chicago and about to nip across the bottom of Lake Michigan? It felt like the country and airline were playing a vast detective game with me: Guess where you are.

We spent half an hour just flying over water, then ten minutes over land, and another twenty minutes over water again. Water edge cities flashed by, ships plied their wares back and forth. That settled it for me: Superior and Huron. But who knew? The airline wasn't letting on, and the country kept its secret close to its chest.

I looked around the aircraft. There was diddly squat leg room, bags were jammed in every crevice available but despite this people were settled and busy. Everyone had their heads down, watching the news on the $3.99 per trip TV pay option, or maybe editing documents on their laptops. Some self-consciously watched a movie on their iPads, others worked through emails offline, or read e-books. A few had their neck pillows firmly in place, shoes slipped off and flights socks on. Most had their own drinks and snacks. Virtually to a man (and woman), window blinds were down. I seemed to be the only one looking out and soaking in the astonishing view.

From there, we headed across the Appalachians toward Newark, and I settled back, taking in the towns and villages lazily strung along valleys, and spotting chi-chi weekender and commuter locations. One tiny place appeared to sport five golf courses, but there didn't seem to be enough housing to support one course, let alone five. A truly astonishing statement of wealth, though clearly not the place to be if golf bored you witless. What would you do all day?

As the sun started to set behind the plane, and

we chased the oblivion of darkness ahead, villages merged into towns, and towns into Jersey and Manhattan's solid commuter heartland. Tails of traffic headed home, street lights picked out the street patterns like a spiders' web lit by torch light, and the Friday evening habits of suburban America became clear. On what seemed like every other corner, baseball and football pitches blazed out activity. Triangles and rectangles, often side by side. Little blocks of players. School teams. Vast arc lights. Sometimes empty stands (practice?), sometimes large crowds. Up in the plane everyone busily got on with being busy, emails, presentations, letters, applications, communicating, and down below they did too. Diligent, active, making the most of chances. The habits of a nation.

There are times when you can fall in love with a country, and this was one of them. I decided that, if I were ever to have a bucket list, I'd just achieved one of the top items - to fly across a country, on a cloudless day, just to see what it looked like from above.

Chapter 12

So here we are, on one of those commuter links out of the bright lights of Manhattan. As we travel beyond the airports' industrial hinterland along the I-78, and approach the cute, neat wooden houses of the Garden State, we shop for nice wine and beautiful flowers to take as gifts.

Nothing, 'though, prepares us for the huge dose of southern hospitality that greets us on our arrival. We are treated to several warm, laughing hours spent with Arlene, her husband, and their teenagers, one in his final year before college, and a daughter two years younger. We sample waldorf salad, alligator and sweet potatoes in just the hottest Cajun sauce, and soft-shell crabs. The food dances on my taste buds, and I am blown away by the quality of Arlene's New Orleans cooking. She is definitely working to make a good impression, and to treat us to the highest level of hospitality, right down to sourcing the out-of-season crabs. As we talk high-school football, college applications, and just about everything else that spring naturally to mind, I wonder at the person who has achieved all of this, and what it takes to do this. It is more than a little humbling.

Arlene's children have been well brought up, are courteous and engaging, and like all teenagers, desperate to get back to social networking, homework, and whatever else is currently taking their fancy. So, after welcoming us into the bosom of their family, they disappear off, and Arlene's husband discretely withdraws to his snug.

"That was amazing, Arlene. Stunningly delicious food. Thank you so much."

"Thank you Teddi. It's my pleasure, and, you know, I like to relax over good food after a hard day's work."

"It's also a pleasure, after so much time on the road. Good home cooking." This from Tad.

"Sounds like you've been through a slog in terms of site visits, Tad"

"Yes I have. And of course you have to be extremely discreet, at the same time. I'm looking forward to going home, Teddi."

"Can I ask you a question?"

"Sure, though whether I can answer is probably an open point."

"The other day, you were talking about the plant we have just seen, and the cost of getting it up to the standard we have promised our investors. Was it all bad?"

Tad visibly relaxes. "No, it wasn't. The workforce itself was extremely productive and efficient, and producing to a high standard. That is actually a major asset, which has to be weighed when considering investing cash into updating the physical facilities."

"So how do you decide how to rationalize production, then? There are a multiplicity of sites, each with pros and cons, both theirs and ours. I mean, it costs to close something down, doesn't it. Some sites can have little short term resale value if they are polluted, or they can have a good one if in a good area and the ground is clean, or cleanable. How do you assess and present?"

I'm asking a pointed question, and deliberately so, given the exchange between Tad and Brett back at the hotel the other day. Arlene looks at me with a very strange look in her eye and it strikes me that she arranged this meal so that we could all talk offline, in precisely this way.

Smart lady.

"Teddi, it depends upon the factors that the investors choose to measure a business by. Do they want maximum dividends now, in which case is cash extremely tight? Do they want reasonable dividends, but also want long term investment and positioning. In which case, the use of cash could differ and there is likely to be more investment in research. If the business is really being challenged to think long term, then the research spend won't just be on tailoring existing know-how to new customers, but also in creating brand new base innovation, the once-in-a-generation breakthroughs that are the lifeblood of a manufacturing business. So that is one way in which the 'big picture' strategy of a business impacts individual commercial decisions. But, it isn't the only way. It will also depend upon things like how we see global markets developing. For example, does a business maximize Asia Pacific or Latin American growth opportunities by building a complete factory? And even if it chooses to build a new factory, where does it choose? China, for example, is an expensive place to manufacture these days, so would a business choose, say, The Philippines or somewhere else? And what is lost, in terms of the producing, lean, efficient workforce that is already in situ in other locations – is the trade-off worth it? How much will it cost to close a facility, and how easy is it? These sorts of issues are on the table before you even begin to consider what to do with a specific site."

There is a short silence.

"So, how do you think it will fall out, Tad? What will the combined business do with all of the sites?"

Another silence. Tad reaches for his wine glass, and I decide to mirror him, to see what happens. Arlene joins in. He looks at us, and it becomes apparent that he knows that his discussion with Brett is the root cause of this discussion now.

"We start by deciding what the factors will be upon which to make a decision. I think that *Brett* is coming under pressure from Gus to cull more of our sites than theirs – after all, a joint venture is a very clear way to kill off a competitors' capability: if the joint venture fails, what has the competitor got left to fall back on? The market is open for the surviving business, for which read technology." He sees me look at him, slightly open-mouthed. "Yes, Teddi, technology. Close sites and you close down the link to manufacturing that ground-breaking research thrives upon. The research dwindles; it gets phased out; the surviving technology dominates. Mergers can simply be a way to destroy your competition."

"What about the synergy of combining technology?"

"That is the holy grail. Combine the businesses so seamlessly and so fast that there is no technological separateness and the joint venture can't fail. Takes that element of risk off the table, and at the same time should deliver the returns that you have agreed with your investors. That's the idea, anyway" He smiles.

"And the sites?"

"Well, we need to get the decision-making factors agreed. We've done most of the research, just a few more visits are left now. I'm not sure how it will all fall out, yet, though I have my own views."

He sees us looking at him and smiles, acknowledging that his attempt to deflect our attention hasn't worked and we won't rest until he gives a little more.

"For what it is worth, my take so far is that we close the French and Italian facilities (both theirs and ours) and supply from our factory in Romania. We continue in the UK as the site there is efficient and highly competitive in terms of costs. There are three distribution centres and five factories in the USA between us, which will need sorting out, but they are efficient so I would like to see centres of excellence develop. We ramp up the Hong Kong distribution terminal to meet Asia Pacific need. The Kingdom business really doesn't need a factory sited there, though some of the local General Managers would no doubt love one to big themselves up. I'd like to streamline their German facility also, keep the differentiation but remove all of the excess and replication. Johann says some of the local finance directors are likely to wave flags around on costs – say that tax prevents that. What do you know of that?"

Both Tad and Arlene look at me. This time I reach for a glass of wine first.

"Well that isn't true, Tad. It's kind of an urban myth. A business can close what it likes from a tax perspective, but when it does so it may incur an upfront tax bill in that country. There are ways that this can be addressed, though the most likely outcome is a deferral in closure, perhaps ten or fifteen years in the worst case scenario."

"So why do they say we can't do it?"

"It's a common blocking ruse, Tad. Deployed to

throw a spanner in the works. Often succeeds too – folks think that it is too much like hard work and focus their attention elsewhere, or at least put off the decision for a while."

There is silence as this sinks in.

"Well that is a shame. What I really want to create is efficient production and research, in co-located centres of excellence. What I don't want is polarized discussion, with status grabs by country chiefs anxious to protect and enhance their fiefdoms."

Whoa, what is *that* all about? Tad looks and sounds unhappy. I'm wondering whether we are touching on delicate ground, perhaps this is resonating with some prior decisions he has made or experiences he has been having recently?

"What you need to focus on, Tad, is that decisions to close factories, or change working practices, are commercial decisions taken by the management team. Period. The job of the finance and tax folks is to work hard to deliver whatever you decide."

Arlene, bless her, closes the thought and wraps it into a reassuring framework for Tad. He looks relieved.

"I think you just hit the nail on the head, Arlene, and thank you."

Chapter 13

The day after finds me heading back to Geneva from Newark Liberty. I'm in Terminal C, and my flight is due to take off from Gate 110, so I've bagged myself a window seat in a diner to gaze across the tarmac at the skyline of Manhattan. A great bit of tourist rubbernecking, and all for the price of a cheeseburger and diet coke.

I'm up for another of those falling-in-love-with-a-country moments. I'm still high from dining with Arlene and her family, but as I gaze across the haze of jet engine exhausts the undercurrents from the last few days drift up through my consciousness.

This merger is all about creating value, but just what is value? Is it the people without a job, or even those who have never had one? Is it city 'scapes blighted by emptied and derelict factories? Or farmland blighted by overuse? For the first time I realize just how hard a job Tad must have, but at the same time, it just seems that there is a vast disconnect between the decisions that individual businesses take and the needs of a host country. When a business closes one factory and opens a new facility with a cheaper workforce or cheaper raw materials, the business can get a real advantage over its competitors. But, they will all follow suit, and soon the costs in the new location will rise. Then what does the business do, look for another cheap location, and repeat the whole exercise? Surely, eventually, the 'cheap' options disappear?

When you stand back and take a good hard look, is it all really a nil sum game? Would a longer view change decisions made, as Tads' comments seemed to suggest? Should a business just not bother? Would its investors really run away hard, until the leveling out took place? Is ten years really an impossible investment period to contemplate? And what about all of the host nations used and abandoned along the way? How do national governments plan to meet their citizens healthcare and schooling needs when they have no idea of the shape of their economy ten years hence?

My head starts to hurt, though I can't tell anymore whether it is exhaustion, an overdose of reality, or caffeine and saturated fats causing my overwrought thoughts. I give up on staring at Manhattan and wander out towards the gate. This time I don't shop.

Chapter 14

Next up is Tad. It's now January, just over a year after we started to work this project, and we are to visit a plant outside of Krakow, ostensibly to do the same as in Philly, but really to finalise positions so the deal could be put forward to the Board. Knowing this, Tad had suggested that we join him and his family for supper on the night before we all flew back out to our respective home countries.

This is to be the home strait for the project. We are finalizing all that we know about one another's businesses, and using the results to negotiate any changes to our initial agreement with one another.

Arlene and I have been working with an international firm of advisers since Philly. When I'd landed back in Geneva, I'd rung her to thank her for dinner. Truth be told, I needed to chew the fat on what had happened over dinner with Tad. He had been open about his views, but his tensions with Brett worried me, as did his outburst about internal politics. I was wondering what the impact could be on the rest of us, and what we could do to pre-empt this. So far, Arlene had come up trumps, been someone I could really talk with, and I was hoping she would this time, too.

"Hey Arlene, it's Teddi."

"Teddi, lovely to hear from you. Are you back

in Geneva yet or still in transit?"

It's the middle of the afternoon in Geneva. The plane got in at five to eight in the morning, and though I was keen to speak with Arlene I knew that I'd get creamed if I rang her in the early hours, New Jersey time. Christoph had met me, taken me to back to my apartment, and generally distracted me for the last few hours. Mmmn.

"Back in Geneva a few hours ago and trying to sort out my unpacking before jet lag hits. I always prefer to travel against the clock, travelling with it just messes up my sleep."

"Well you have been away for a while now, haven't you?"

"Far too long." I laugh, and she joins in. "Listen Arlene, I just wanted to thank you one more time for dinner the other evening. It really was truly kind of you and I felt very welcome."

"Teddi it was our pleasure. I have to say that I was a little worried about Tad, by the end of dinner."

Bless her. As usual, she gets the point. It's like she reads my mind. Or maybe, just maybe, we are thinking alike. Maybe she needs to talk with me as much as I need to talk with her.

"Funny you should mention that. I've been mulling over what he said, trying to think about implications, consequences, impacts. You know, whether there is anything that we need to be doing differently?"

"To our specific plans for each country?"

"That's right. But also, what to do about the pressure from Gus on Brett."

"Like call in external lawyers or accountants to help us in some way? Hasn't Brett said we can't have that budget?"

"Yes he has. But, and this is a huge but, the

Board would normally expect the team to benchmark their thinking as part of the process of preparing a paper for Board review. Which means spend some money on external advisers. Maybe we could bring that forward, incorporate it in some way into our work in the next few months?"

"I like your thinking, Teddi. It will ensure that the plans have a solid base because there will be an opinion from the advisers, but it will also help Tad and Brett push back on Gus. It's not illogical, after all, and it's a big transaction - no-one wants to discover that a huge amount of work is needed, or even a change in direction, when they're about to go to the Board. I can see only one problem - where do we get the cash from to pay for this? Brett is tight with cash."

"Well just as an aside, and between you and I, I'm not so sure he *is* tight with cash. There seems to be a lot of flying around the place in business class and staying in top-class hotels. But let's put that to one side for now. I am wondering whether Hans, as our Group Head of Tax, has a budget for this kind of thing. After all, meeting this need must happen all the time, so it must be paid for somehow? Maybe there could be room for manoeuvre there, or at least he could apply pressure to open up the coffers?"

"Well I'm in the same boat as you on this, Teddi. I don't know how this is done, but I do have a suggestion. I'll talk with the guys here that I know have pushed a Board paper forward before, and see if there is a known way forward."

"Well I can try the same. If you let me know what you find out Arlene, I could then make the approach to Hans?"

"Sounds like a plan to me" and she had laughed.

True to her word, she had done exactly that, and

taking my cue from her, I'd discussed the issue with the finance leads from one or two other major subsidiaries, including Australia, the home of Wildcat's headquarters. Within a week I had talked with Hans. Somehow that conversation, together with behind the scenes pressure applied from Arlene's end, and those other leads, had produced a turnaround in Brett's approach. We had been able to engage advisers.

Which had been hugely beneficial to the project, as Arlene and I had been able to benchmark our ideas with these guys, and indeed they had been able to suggest improvements. We even had them test the underlying numbers, putting the data through powerful analysis and producing robust support that they felt comfortable standing behind.

It wasn't so beneficial to my airline frequent flyer accounts, it had to be said. The guys in the Australian office of our advisers were well used to dealing with international business, and more than happy to hold conference calls at the end of their working day (and the start of ours).

So, I hadn't needed to travel, 'though truth be told, I'd felt better for that. Our discussions with Tad and the reality of factory closure that I had seen in Philly had begun to hit home. The way money was being spent left, right and centre on deal costs was beginning to unnerve me. Technology was invented to make life easier, and a few conference calls and video calls were far cheaper than a return business class ticket to Australia. I became adept at taking and making calls with Asia Pacific in the morning, and with the Americas after lunch. I turned my back on once-tantalising offers of trips and substituted them with video-conference calls at odd hours. Only occasionally, when a face to face negotiation just had to be held, or a vast volume of paperwork trawled through, did Arlene and I need to put bums on seat.

It was enlightening how few trips were truly needed.

Chapter 15

So, this time, it is the turn of Arlene and I to catch a taxi from our hotel and head out into an unfamiliar landscape. The reception is just as warm as last time, though; this time from Tad's wife, Beata, a computer programmer, and their two little girls (until they get shepherded off sleepy yet protesting, to bed). I fall in love with Beata's rosol, a kind of chicken soup with noodles, Arlene with the cutlet that followed, and both of us drink more vodka than is sensible for a beginner. Through the evening, Beata regales us with tales of the expat bosses she has worked for since graduating from university, Tad with stories of Poland after escape from communist rule, and both with the kind of minutiae of small town life that we all know well from our childhood years.

Beata and Tad clear the table and serve up coffee. An attempt to help us sober up, our flights tomorrow would be a vomit-comet killer otherwise.

"Well, that was fabulous, Beata. Thank you so much."

"Thank you. We thought that you might like to try some traditional dishes. I hope that they weren't too unusual?"

"You know, my husband and I took a trip around Europe a couple of years ago, on the back of a trip I had to make to Geneva. The cutlets reminded me of something we had in Vienna, viener schnitzel it was called. Could they be the same?"

"Arlene, I think they have the same derivation, somewhere back along the line in our history." Tad is relaxed now, positively loquacious, and with none of the anxiety displayed when we were at Arlene's house. It's not a surprise. We have managed to complete our work, with no real changes, but with all the loose ends checked out and tied down, and all of us are feeling relieved. Final signature on the deal can't be too far off now.

"The question I have, though", Tad is continuing, "is what Teddi will choose to serve us when she invites us over to her place. After all, it's her turn next." With which he breaks into laughter, and they all join in.

I'm a little non-plussed, but then I realize that this was on the cards all along. What else can you do but smile, wryly?

"Do you know, it's as much about where I host dinner for you as what? We could meet in Geneva, where I am posted now, or in London, where I used to live. What do you guys prefer? Opportunity dependent, of course."

There is a short pause. They're thinking about this (through the vodka).

"Well, doesn't it also depend on your family circumstances, Teddi? Do you have family in either location?"

"No family in either, Arlene." Another wry smile. "Though I do have my London family, as I call it. My good friends, best buddies I've known since college, and my support network in times of crisis and celebration. You'd enjoy meeting them."

"It's not the same though, is it?" As ever, the pertinent factual point from Tad. "What about the guy in Geneva?"

This time I really am taken aback. How can they possibly know about Christoph? I've stayed silent about him so far, really tried to keep him hidden from view. Guess I've met their families, and they feel they can ask questions like this. We're friends ourselves, now.

There's no point in staying mum.

I laugh. "So how do you know about him, Tad? I've done my very best to keep him a secret."

"That's not difficult. I've seen him meet you in reception of our building in Geneva. Yes, Teddi, I am often there. Probably every month or so. He looks like a serious deal."

"So who is he, Teddi? Don't hold back."

"Oh man, you guys, what are you like?" I'm laughing now with them, playing up and playing along, before continuing.

"Ok, ok. Here's the lowdown. His name is Christoph Dettwiler. He's a research physicist with the quantum physics boys. We've been dating for almost a year. We don't live together. We do love each other. I'm very happy." And I laugh again, as much out of embarrassment as anything else. I cannot believe I have just fessed up like this. Must be the vodka. Either that or finally this uptight English rose is learning to feel.

What's nice is that they don't laugh, or at least not nastily. More like beaming smiles, happy ones, genuine and *for* me not *at* me.

"That's really wonderful, Teddi. I am genuinely happy for you."

"Me too. Now tell me, is this at the stage where you would introduce him to us?"

"Good question, and a fair one." I sip my coffee,

and contemplate, inwardly, whether I truly know where the relationship stands.

"We spent New Year together (I went home to see my parents at Christmas) with his parents at their home. We spend every weekend together, and some evenings during the week too. He tests me out, every so often, in his conversation, assessing how I feel about big relationship issues like children. I can talk to him like no-one else, he understands me like no-one I have ever known, and he is my greatest friend. We meet intellectually, which is important. I admire and respect him. I love him…." My voice trails off for a moment. This *must* be the vodka, mustn't it? "I think I'd be proud to introduce you to him, to be honest, 'though as my boyfriend only. We aren't engaged."

"And you wouldn't want us to mention it so as not to rock the boat. Don't worry Teddi, we get it."

"Thanks Arlene." I brighten.

"Though I can't promise not to make him understand how great an opportunity you are and how mad he would be to let you pass on by."

"Well, it sounds like we have another dinner to plan, as and when we get the chance. Though I can't promise anything about my cooking." And we all laugh, and another great evening, very entertaining, totally charming, flies by, keeping the bar way high.

Chapter 16

The receiver pings as it settles back onto the cradle, and I nurse my warm ears in relief. Thank goodness that's over. A two hour telephone conference with what felt like half the world, a marathon of explanation, negotiation and compromise.

The aim? To finalise the Board paper for the Kingdom deal. It's the culmination of all our hard work. It explains the deal, all the pros and cons, the risks and benefits, the actions needed, the money that has to be spent, the money that can be saved. It's not the easiest task, either. Trying to encompass months and months of work, and hundreds of pages of detailed reports and advice from a myriad of external experts, all into a seven page summary. It's not the only information that the Board will receive, though, that would be ludicrous. The paper will be presented by Brett who will talk around it and answer questions. There will be a back-up paper with further detail, and they can ask for any further information they want, including copies of the advice from external experts. The purpose of all of this is to enable them to take their decision on a fully informed basis (which is both their job and their prerogative).

Even so, seven pages isn't much. We each fed Brett with the data for our part of the jigsaw. Time, though, slipped by whilst Brett compiled the paper, and it's the end of May before we got together in this call to discuss the changes that we each wanted to make to Brett's words and numbers.

The call quickly devolved down to the red lines that we each adamantly insisted upon. Which wasn't necessarily a bad thing. It brought clarity, though the risk of conflict too. We got that resolved, usually via deft wording from Chip, and occasionally via hard negotiation.

I updated my opinion of Chip during the call. He was always able to find a way to say what needed to be said, often bringing parties together and negotiations to a fruitful conclusion. Very smart. I definitely came away from the call with a whole extra chunk of respect for him (and a whole lot less chippiness besides).

It had been a long call, though, and it was a blessed relief to be able to stand up, walk away from my desk and stretch out.

I needed too as well. Tonight was a big evening for me. It was time to introduce Christoph to Em. Well, it was probably hugely overdue, if I was honest with myself. I'd kept Christoph to myself, hadn't introduced him to anyone in Geneva. We had been seeing each other for over a year now, and I wondered why I hadn't done this sooner. Truth be told, I was just so scared of somehow blowing things. It all seemed so perfect that sometimes I could barely breathe.

Em and I had agreed that keeping the pressure off Christoph somewhat was a good idea (though maybe it was really for my benefit?), and she had suggested that we met up in a group. So, tonight, we are keeping it casual and joining a gaggle of expat buddies.

They're a good group, always roving and

rotating around one another's apartments, and the bars and restaurants in town. Over time, old faces disappear onto another posting (always bidden a fond farewell with exchange of contact data) and new faces arrive. It is the endless merry-go-round of expat life, with its succession of often shallow acquaintances. Surviving-a-lifetime friendships are as rare as hen's teeth, but it felt that mine with Em would be one of those. Tonight, though, we are out with the wider gaggle.

Christoph and I walk into the bar. He's looking pretty good tonight, it has to be said. He's wearing a dark suit and open necked shirt. The suit looks tailored to fit, as does the shirt. Discreet though, not even remotely glamorous or to-the-minute fashionable. Covered buttons, hand stitching, a flattering cut, the shirt cuff revealed just-so. The subtle hallmarks of a bespoke suit, nothing off the peg. It isn't a suit I have seen before, either. It suddenly occurs to me that maybe he is as keen to make tonight work as I am, a thought which suddenly makes me feel all squirmy and warm inside.

"Teddi!"

I'd know that voice anywhere.

"Em! Hi, hi."

We air kiss.

"Em, could I introduce Christoph Dettwiler? Christoph, please meet my good friend Maertje van den Bos. Em for short."

They shake hands.

"Pleased to meet you, Em."

"You too, Christoph. Heard a lot about you. All good of course."

They're smiling and laughing. Phew. The first stage is over, and seems to have gone well. My shoulders relax with relief.

Em carries on, introducing the crowd to Christoph, and then she drags us over to two new faces who are hanging back from the mob. The guy looks oddly familiar, and as we walk over I madly try to rack my brains to see how I might know him.

He's not from the office. I've not had any drunken, one-night, after hours fumbles through beer goggles whilst in Geneva (not my style, anyway). I'm wondering whether I know him, and what embarrassing revelation could be in store when Em makes the introductions.

"Teddi, Christoph, meet Erik, my brother, and his English wife, Katie."

Light dawns. He's Em's brother! He's a whole lot broader, though with a wingers' physique rather than a prop forwards', and despite the huge shoulders and muscular solidity I can see nuances of Em: the eyes, evenly set and green with hazel glints, the way their smiles curve up at the ends, and those knowing looks to one another that come from long-standing shared jokes and experiences.

From there on in, the evening starts to run very smoothly. Erik used to play rugby, but is a marine biologist. It turns out that he is a keen diver, like Christoph, and they suddenly develop a lengthy conversation comparing dive sites around the world. We've bought a second round, but they barely break their conversation to put down empties and pick up new supplies. Em, Katie and I are thrown together.

We swap a few stories before we get onto those dread questions of any middle-class social conversation:

"What do you do?"

"Where do you live?"

"Where did you do your MBA?"

Or, maybe, "Which school do your children attend?" (if you have them).

But the questions don't follow the dread pattern this time, and I rapidly feel utterly ashamed of such shallow thoughts.

"I was made redundant a couple of years ago. I've held a couple of temp positions since then, but a permanent one is just impossible to land. They're just not around. When they do appear, there are so many people applying that landing even a polite refusal seems impossible, let alone an interview…"

He voice trails off. She looks downcast, as what was clearly a thin veneer of jolly-jolly bonhomie slips away.

"Oh, I'm sorry. How tactless of me. How are you coping?"

Katie's eyes well up, but she looks steadily at me as her eyes blur, holding my gaze. I stay silent, in listening mode, and let her decide how to respond. After a few moments, and a long hug from Em which doesn't look to be the first, she swallows and smiles.

"I'm not, truth be told. It's a terrible situation. I feel like I'm on the scrapheap. I feel invisible."

How so? She doesn't seem old enough for that. It's something that I associate with redundancies of middle managers in their late fifties. She looks to be in her late thirties. How can this be so?

"So what do you normally do? What were you doing before all this happened?"

"Well, I used to head up an internal law team." She mentions a major household name and we all nod, sagely; during the recession they've been in the news making cut after cut.

"They decided to set up a shared services office in another European country where labour is far cheaper," she continues. "A lot of our work was shifted there, and what we were left with meant that our team had to be "right-sized." One of my middle managers ended up running a small team of what would be, basically, project managers. Wasn't just my team, either. Accounts were affected. The Buyers team. IT. Lots of teams, actually" she shrugs.

"Lots of people deemed surplus to requirements," she adds quietly.

"The thing is, there are now so many educated, qualified people who have lost their jobs sloshing around the jobs market that when a role does come up, the HR team concerned is just inundated with CVs. Even at my level they can get fifty or sixty CVs, you know.

Of course, it's impossible for them to give enough time to thoroughly consider each application. They're forced into sifting, often dumping an application on the most spurious grounds. A candidate could be the best thing since sliced bread, but that doesn't matter. They just don't have time to really contemplate the applicant behind the application, and of course there are applicants with such varied ages and experiences that they can pick and choose."

She looks sad, but even despite this is being very decent, and very British, I think, by being so very fair on the CV sifters. She also looks a little relieved. Maybe saying all this gets it off her chest, helps in some way.

"I've been told that looking for a new role can be a job in itself."

That isn't *totally* true. I actually read it in a newspaper column, but it may get her talking again.

"Oh, you spend hours, days, weeks, on a major

application. Researching, giving your CV a new twist, filling forms, online psychometric tests, travelling to and attending interviews, often a sequence of three or four involving interview panels and presentations and all sorts of things. When you add it up, you may well have quite literally devoted three or four weeks to an application that ultimately goes nowhere."

She pauses, before carrying on (a little more steadily and confidently).

"The irony is, you no longer have the childcare, or the cleaner, or the ironer or the dog walker. You end up trying to job-hunt full time, and be an old-fashioned housewife, all in the hours between start and end of school. It's actually quite schizophrenic."

She smiles, and this time it reaches her eyes.

"But you manage. You learn how to allocate your week," she adds.

"I'm very proud of Katie," puts in Em. "I don't know how you managed to hold it all together. Keep the family afloat. Keep your finances afloat, too."

Em, bless her. Ever so supportive.

"How have you managed?"

"Being very careful," she shrugs, before continuing. "Shop for food at the discount supermarkets and stores. Sell clothes we've used on the internet. Buy second hand toys for the kids. Dump the private school. Spend savings. Get reading books from the library. Avoid supermarket supposed special offers like the plague. Drive your car into the ground and not replace it until it dies. You would be amazed how you can make things stretch."

It's quite impressive. Real ingenuity. Having said that, I can't say I want to be in her shoes.

Stretching can only take you so far, and there must come a point beyond which matters become really quite grave indeed.

"That is seriously impressive."

"Thanks. It helps that Erik has just had a promotion. And that we have a fab sister in Maertje, who invites us on a weekend break to Geneva using her airline frequent flyer account."

We all laugh in support and agreement.

"Have you thought of an alternative career route?"

"Yes, actually. Looked at teaching but I don't want to have to go back to University for two years. I mean, I have a degree. And a post-graduate qualification. But, you can't just switch over, you have to do a subject refresher for a year then a year of teacher training. Which also means both not earning and shelling out tuition fees. Not on the cards!

"I've looked at roles more junior than the one I had, but you don't get taken seriously. I'm fed up with being told that the hirer has decided to focus on the less-experienced market – which can range from anything to age discrimination to refusing to let you price compete. I've looked at general job sites for fill-in work, you know temporary hires in the run up to Christmas, call centres, that sort of thing. Even that is impossible. You have to have current, relevant experience. It's a nightmare."

"Katie's had a great idea, though," Em adds.

"Thanks." She looks a little embarrassed, so Em continues. "She's doing some brush up work and aims to shift sectors. She's got bags of transferrable skills. Any business would be lucky to have her."

"Sounds like a plan." And it does. But it's all still very sobering. Behind the careful plans are dashed hopes, and self-belief battered time and time again. The reality of redundancy is ever more clearly enunciated.

"Really wish you well." I mean it. "Cheers!" we toast, at which point Erik and Christoph suddenly reappear in our conversation again. Maybe they had noticed our more intimate conversation, and had been waiting for a suitable moment to rejoin us?

"So, girls, this looks fun. What are up to next, Sis? Where are we going next tonight?"

Erik injects a dose of levity, and before we know it we are wrapped up in the expat mob and heading to someone's apartment for nibbles. It's three hours later before we all say our goodbyes and Christoph and I finally get time on our own again.

We're wrapped up in one another's arms, and slowly strolling back to my place, which isn't too far away.

"So what happened back at the bar, Teddi?"

I know immediately what he is referring to. As we slowly walk, we talk too, and gradually Christoph gets to hear of Katie's private pain. I stay mute about my own growing concerns about the human impact of corporate decisions.

Chapter 17

I'm just opening an email with huge attachments – the prepared Board paper, courtesy of Brett and Armand's PA – when Em appears at my office door.

"Morning, Teddi."

"Morning. Em."

"Coffee?"

"Mmmn. Gotta be quick, though. Got a meeting at ten. That ok?"

"Sure."

"Ok then, just let me print and save this email, then I'm good to go."

To be honest, I don't need a coffee right now, and need a distracting break even less. It's Monday morning, no time to be hanging around. I want to keep this short, and make it look like a meeting, so will drag Em back to my office with our coffees to sit at my desk. But, and this is a huge but, Em doesn't normally appear at my desk at quarter past nine on any day, and certainly not on a Monday, She's even more of a workaholic than I am, probably more so, so this doesn't bode well.

We're walking along the corridor.

"So, what's up?"

Straight to the point. Can't see any purpose in beating about the bush.

"Erik and Katie still with you?" I add. At a

guess, some element of their visit must be what's playing on her mind.

"They're heading out to the airport today."

Wow, still not at her most communicative.

"Come on, Em. What's on your mind?"

She takes a deep breath.

"Well what do *you* think?"

Slightly sharp. Unnecessarily so I initially think, but there again I don't know what is going on with her. Suspect the question is rhetorical.

"Things are really rough for them. You have no idea…." Her voice, normally direct and clear, fades away. "I've never seen them like this. There was a lot of acting on Friday evening, you know. Not having a job is killing Katie. The financial strain is enormous. And the weight on Erik – he has aged, believe me he has aged."

"Come on." I drag her back to my office with our coffees and close the door.

"Right, what exactly is Katie's position? I couldn't enquire too closely on Friday."

"Savings mostly gone. Has this idea to reposition herself, though I don't think her heart is in it. And they need to get it done while they still can pay for it. Self-confidence battered. The London job market is absolutely terrible."

"How does she explain the gap on her CV?"

"They've had a child, so now they have two, so she calls it a career break. Though that is sugar coating reality, as we know. And the switch will be explainable – she can say she needs to step off the senior job rung of the career ladder for her family, and this enables her to contribute her vast experience yet manage that also. It's not so bad, as things go."

"Though the pay would be somewhat lower than she is used to?"

"Far higher than her current situation…."

"Fair comment."

We drift into silence.

"Do you ever wonder about us, Teddi?"

Ah, so this is the crux of the issue.

"Us?"

"Look at us. We each left our jobs behind to come here on an expat package. Our jobs back home have long been filled. Any cost-cutting exercise here at global head office could leave you and I high and dry. Have you ever wondered what would happen then? Do you ever feel vulnerable?"

"To be honest, when I first came here I didn't think about that for a moment. But being fair, I've started to notice the negative consequences of corporate decisions. You know, what happens after a factory closes, the personal impacts for people like Katie, so, do I think about it? Yeah. Thinking about it and starting to have real misgivings. Hadn't really focused on my own situation, but now you mention it, can't say I'm feeling good about that either. Or maybe I have contemplated it but I'm in denial."

I look at her.

"Can't say I have an action plan in place, 'though. How 'bout you?"

"No, none, same as you." She shakes her head. "But I'm beginning to wonder whether I should."

There's some truth in this, somewhere.

"Well to allow that to dominate your behaviour is to succumb to negative thinking, and that just isn't you, Em."

She smiles. "Nor you."

"But worth maybe getting some feelers out into the job market?"

"Assuming you don't get found out."

She's right there too. The local job market has

stagnated slightly. There are worries that US headquartered businesses may pull out, and retrench back to the US. People aren't moving around, and there are the war stories (possibly urban myths) of people losing their jobs after their HR team found out that they were casing the job market. Pretty shitty if true.

"Well, don't know about you, but I'm not able to decide on that right now, and I do have a ten o'clock to get to. But it's food for thought, Em, food for thought."

At which we part, and I head off to my meeting with an emptiness in my stomach that I haven't felt since the airport at Newark.

Chapter 18

Yay! Barely five days go by and we get the news that everyone working on the Kingdom deal has been waiting for. The Board has approved the deal, and we can progress with getting it in place.

I've called into the office on Saturday morning. Christoph has had to head to the lab, so I've gone in to clear my inbox backlog. There, waiting for me is an email from Amand and Brett's PA, copied to the team and a lot of others as well, attaching the signed Board paper.

Fabulous! I forward the email to Tad and Arlene together with a suitably upbeat message, and print it off and save it, as is my habit. I'm just settling down to scan it and see whether they have made any changes, which sometimes happens, when another email pops into my inbox, also from Armand's PA. It's attaching the paper, again, which I print and save, again again.

Then I look bewildered at the three piles of paper on my desk. One from Brett on Monday, and two from Amand's PA today. That's a lot of line by line scanning.

I go to get a coffee. This isn't going to be quick.

Sure enough, it isn't. It's a whole two hours later before I look up and stare ahead. What I have just read cannot make sense. The second copy from Amand's PA matches Monday's one from

Brett perfectly. Word for word. But the first one from his PA? Now that is a whole new ball of wax. Radically different. In fact forget that, it is wildly, radically different. Different numbers. Different recommendations. Different conclusions.

What the hell is it?

I look at my inbox again, as if it has all been a dream and this will prove it. But, no, there they are, the two from Amand's PA. However, that's not all that is there. I notice that she has sent out a recall on the first email. It hasn't worked (I'd already opened it) but I pause. This still doesn't make sense, but some quiet voice inside tells me to print and save the recall note as well, and then to beat a hasty retreat from the office with all of my paper copies.

Someone didn't want us to see that first email.

I need to think this one through.

Chapter 19

I'm sat at my dining table, with the glorious warmth of early June sunshine beating its way through the shutters on the windows. In any other circumstance I would be heading outside, lured by the siren call of summer, but not today.

I've repeatedly looked over the two sets of attachments sent by Armand and Brett's PA. Oddly, the second Board paper isn't signed, the one that dovetails with what we were expecting to see. From what I understand, they usually appear back with the scrawls of various Board members appended at the bottom, and whilst this is certainly the case for the first one, the one that was waiting for me in my inbox this morning, it isn't for the one that followed.

As if reading my thoughts, we receive yet another email, this from Brett, apologizing for sending out the unsigned version of the approved Paper, and promising to attach it for our kind attention. He's forwarding his PA's second email, and he explains further that their PA was suddenly taken ill in the week and this was sent by a temp. Lo and behold, he then forwards on a copy of the second paper, this time with signatures.

This all seems to make sense, assuming that you don't know about the existence of the first email from the temp. After all, he's explaining the mix up and making prompt amends. However, assuming that you do know about the other paper, then this flurry of activity just adds to the already confused picture (and it doesn't explain why two papers exist in the first place.)

Looks like Brett is keen to reinforce the picture painted by the second set of papers, but the first now both intrigues and scares me.

The changes aren't mere typos, such as spelling mistakes. They aren't careless, over-tired errors, such as repeated cut 'n' paste sections.

This is a fundamental rewrite. It's talking about closing factories that we recommended should stay open (and more of them, too). It rips up the distribution footprint. It slashes research – in fact it doesn't just slash research, it cuts its jugular. This isn't a blueprint for growth and investment, it's a slash 'n' burn, short-termist cash grab, and fuelled by debt at that.

I feel sick, comprehensively gutted in fact. I need a break, so store the papers away and go for a run. It's not until I'm pounding along the hot tarmac at a rattlingly good pace that I realize that I am panicking, too.

That paper had signatures on it. It wasn't just some background thought piece outlining alternatives, the sort of thing that can appear during a deal, but not at the end.

I suddenly stop, as if winded.

Shit!

Just which paper *did* the Board approve?

Chapter 20

Having discovered a situation like this, what do you do? There is no doubt that you need to do something, but how do you raise your concerns? What are the legal issues in doing so, and who do you talk to? Has the Board of a major quoted business had the wool pulled over its eyes? Has it actually chosen to behave like this? Or are there material facts of which you aren't aware such that the decision makes a whole lot more sense?

I've spent the last two weeks getting virtually no sleep, sweating through the night trying to work out where to start and who the hell I talk to when I do. Christoph and I don't live together (I'm way too old-fashioned for that), so he hasn't been privy to this nightly torment. But he has noticed how tired I am, absent minded, not really all there when we meet for dinner, or to go to the theatre.

"Teddi, is anything the matter?"

We are in a taxi heading back to my place, after a subdued quiet Saturday evening dinner. I've been atrocious company and I look a mess.

"Teddi, is there something I need to know? Are we ok?"

Oh bless him. He thinks this is about us.

"No Christoph, nothing wrong with us. I'm just tired, is all. I have that trip to London tomorrow, remember?"

"But you've never seemed tired ahead of a trip before."

He is quite correct, of course. I'm worried because it's the first time I'll be face to face with the team, including with Brett, since that crazy Saturday two weeks ago and its barrage of emails. I still haven't formulated a firm way forward: thinking about approaching Hans, on a confidential basis, but what can he achieve? He received the papers himself, anyway.

And what are other people thinking? Have they even noticed? Or am I the only person who isn't in on the whole rationale for the unusual version? And what will it mean for me, once I do raise it? Quietly sidelined? Counseled out? Or maybe labeled as a whistle blower, resorting to employment tribunals to seek the compensation that I'll never earn now? All that hard work, and for what?

"Christoph," I begin, and I pause. I can't tell him the facts, as that would break in-house confidentiality rules. "There is something going on that is worrying me stupid. I can't tell you the facts, but I know I need to do something though I don't know what."

"This is serious?"

"Yes."

"If it were something at the lab, affecting me, in my world, how would you describe it?"

That's a good idea. Putting it in the world of experimental physicists will at least give Christoph an inkling of what I am dealing with.

"Christoph, let's just say, hypothetically, that you conclude your current set of experiments, and you draft a paper describing the work, the findings, and conclusions to be drawn from that. You put it forward for review from the rest of the team before you all publish it. When you get the authorized copy back you find that the findings and conclusions have changed, even the factual focus. You barely recognize the paper, but it has your name on it (and the rest of the teams' come to that). What would you do, hypothetically speaking?"

Christoph looks at me, quite dumbfounded.

"That wouldn't happen."

"I didn't say it would. It's a hypothetical example. Go on, how would you respond? What would be your gut reaction?"

"I guess I would want to raise the issue, before the paper came out."

"Who would you raise it with? In this hypothetical example the folks you would raise it with, your co-researchers and line managers as it were, are the ones who appear to have made the changes."

"I guess there must be someone else I could approach. A regulatory body maybe." Then he pauses, and looks steadily for a moment or two, eyes downcast. He looks up. "Probably my first port of call would be someone discreet, in the loop, yet removed from the minutiae. Probably someone highly respected in the organization, yet sufficiently independent-minded. Probably also with an enquiring mind – what has happened? – rather than finger pointing. Seeking enlightenment in the first instance."

He pauses and looks at me. It's probably a fair assessment of the situation, if only he knew it.

"I'll take that on board. Wise words, Christoph. Thank you." And I smile back the tears that threaten to overwhelm me. "You know me, I'm a bit of a worrier. It's probably all a storm in a teacup." And I try to lightly laugh it all off.

Christoph smiles too, but his brown eyes remain serious, not quite convinced, and his love-making later is urgent yet tender.

Chapter 21

Late on Sunday afternoon I find myself sharing a car out to Geneva International Airport with Guillame, our Global Director of Intellectual Property. I've got some serious respect for this guy; he really knows his subject matter inside and out, is sharp as a tack bright, but is also a very decent, courteous person. No side, never struck me as one of those people who walk away from a call or meeting and immediately start to stab you in the back.

He was recruited from GOIP, the Global Organisation for Intellectual Property, in what at the time was widely regarded as a bit of a coup. The founding Treaty had been signed in 1968, with the body formally established by 1971. It pulled in talent from around the globe, attracted by working in such a prestigious and exciting environment.

Guillame had joined in the eighties, and immediately his intellect and diplomatic charm had attracted attention. He clearly had the capability to get to the top, and his poaching by our business had been widely admired. Needless to say, he had reached the top at our business, and his uncanny ability to handle any personality was universally admired. By the time he and I met, he had become the ultimate statesman of the business.

So we're driving past the Basilique de Notre

Dame, along the Rue de la Servette, and towards the airport. He's reminding me of a business trip we took together. Our American hosts had taken us to a restaurant for dinner. The time zone gap was pretty horrendous, seven zones in all, and after a day of meetings we were starting to flag. Johann and I hadn't been to that restaurant before, and in our defence didn't notice that we were plainly being egged on to orders starters that no-one else was bothering with. When they arrived, we nearly fell off our chairs – Johann's plate of onion rings was as big as a laptop, and my salad arrived on an oval party platter. Our hosts had roared with laughter, before joining in to eat up and clear the plates. It was a gently funny, warming memory, rather than rip-roaringly hilarious, but we definitely laugh as the car slips along. It's funny how laughter can feel so wonderful, when you have been feeling so down.

I must have lapsed into silence without realizing it, as it dawned, back then, that that was a time when I had been so naïve about the team (well, one member in particular), and the worry of the last two weeks overwhelmed me again.

"Something you would like to share?"

"What?"

"Is there something you would like to share?" He smiles a very kind smile.

"Oh, you wouldn't believe me if I told you" and I try to laugh, as if making light of something potentially humorous.

"Like I said, you wouldn't believe me..." and this time I look him straight in the eye, no smile, and hold the look.

The pause stretches like the elastic on your hold ups, long enough, but won't hold forever.

"Remember the Board paper that we reviewed

and signed off on about three weeks ago?"

"Of course, Teddi."

"Do you have a copy of what was reviewed on the day of the Board meeting, and minuted?"

"It's the same thing …," he raises his eyebrows quizzically.

"Amand's PA was off sick a couple of weeks ago, and her temp sent out the papers and minutes instead. You've seen those?"

"No, I've been on vacation. I think that that block of reading it still in my inbox as a matter of fact. Why do you ask?"

"Well, she sent out two versions, but then tried to recall one of them a couple of hours later. I'd already opened them both, and maybe others had too. Either way, the recall failed and a new email appeared shortly afterwards from Brett with only one version attached."

My voice trails off. We are pulling up to the departures doors of Terminal T1. I look out, and back at Guillame, but he is already climbing out of the Merc.

Oh crap, I think, now I've blown it. Shouldn't have mentioned it. Now what have I done? Shouldn't have let my guard down. Damn those kind eyes (and that clever use kindness). I grab my rollaboard suitcase from the driver, and am about to head in on my own, eyes downcast, when Guillame murmurs something.

"What changed, Teddi?"

Like I said, he is smart.

I take a deep breath. We are walking into the terminal so this has to be fast (as well as quiet).

"As you correctly hint, there is a second paper, also signed, but with wildly different content. The recommendation in that paper is to close both our Newcastle and their Pennsylvania plants, keep open Paris, and make wholesale switches of production to a new plant in Korea; I don't even recognize the data used to support it and it's nothing like the findings that Tad and his counterpart came up with, which clearly pointed to quite radically different decisions."

I pause, before continuing.

"And there is this reference to delivering 12% of the current year PBF by this route, such that 100% will be achieved. I mean, what on earth is *that*? I am totally confused, and extremely worried because that's not what I signed off on. What is going on? Do you have any idea?"

Which was when I realize that he has actually stopped walking and is staring at me, open-mouthed. For a period that feels like the entire rush hour traffic hurtling through the New Jersey turnpike, but is actually maybe a couple of seconds tops, we stand like that, then he visibly pulls himself up.

"Who else knows?"

"Any of the other addressees? Guess it depends upon whether they opened the first email? Maybe the recall didn't work? Often doesn't, particularly cross-border."

"Which means that it could have been read by others before the temp recalled it?" He is looking frighteningly angry now, pure cold fury in his eyes. Very unlike him and
not at all pleasant to behold.

"I guess. I've tried and tried to think who to talk to about this, but when the Global Board makes a decision like that, who do you tell, where do you start? Who do you trust?"

"And you trust me?"

My sagging shoulders and weak attempt at a reassuring smile must make him realize that the answer is yes, and also that I am feeling way exposed by now.

"Just a couple more questions, Teddi" and he looks me straight in the eye again, not even breaking it as he hands his ticket and passport to the airline check-in aide. This time there is no fury. Coldness yes, but smart coldness, fast thinking distance, and more than the faintest hint of determination.

"What about Tad and Arlene? Or Johann or Chip. You talk with those guys regularly. Have you spoken to any of them about this?"

"Nothing formally. I've spent two weeks reviewing my own perspective, to try to decide what to do."

"So anyone else who read this will be working out what they feel is the right thing to do, also?"

"Mmmn, something like that, I guess, though, who knows?"

"One last question."

"OK"

"What did you do with the attachments, once you had opened the emails?"

"Good question – the usual. I opened the email and stored the attachments straight away without reading them. On my personal g:drive and the departmental secure filing area on the shared k:drive. So I guess they're very safe. I didn't realize what was in them until I printed off a copy to read and add to paper files." My voice trailed off.

"So if we multiply that kind of process by the number of recipients, then there is probably an electronic and paper trail a mile wide? The data is secure, but pervasive."

"I guess. And deleting emails or files wouldn't change that, as we both know. Short of grabbing hard drives, and physically destroying them, there is no way to prevent data from being recovered (unless the data has, somehow, been overwritten, which is unlikely in the time frame, and pretty haphazard at any time). An email purge would destroy other corporate records, which you wouldn't want to risk. So, yes, assuming that these have been read and stored, then the data is secure but pervasive, as you point out, and the sender can't easily alter that."

He is looking at me. The desk clerk coughs as if to ask for my documents too, so I hand them over.

"Look, Teddi, obviously I need to review the emails myself – I don't even know if I have both copies yet. I can see that you are worried. Could you give me a chance to look into this? Perhaps two weeks? I'll mention no names, in fact I am as interested in this as you are, perhaps more."

Guess it is some survival mechanism, or maybe just dumb luck, but here is just the kind of person that Christoph had described.

"Guillame, two weeks is fine, I guess. I'd like to think that we could meet up then to review the situation, for you to brief me about what you have found out. Could we do that?"

"Of course, I'll send through a meeting invite"

"Thanks, Guillame, in which case then please do go ahead. Guess the only concern now is what other people could be thinking? And what will happen during the implementation meeting this week in London. How will we handle things?"

"Teddi, you can only do as your conscience dictates. For my part, until I get to the bottom of this, I'm going to proceed as if the Board paper we are to implement was the one that we all reviewed and signed off on. The attempt at recall suggests that some or all of us weren't supposed to see the alternative, so let's proceed on what we know is the basis."

"And if anything untoward happens?"

"That we will have to play by ear. We may not get two weeks Teddi. My suggestion is that if *anything* crops up that we aren't happy about, we should immediately call for a time out. Would you be comfortable with that?"

I nod ok, and with that we head off into the bowels of the airport. True to his word, within ten minutes of arriving in the airport lounge Guillame sends through a meeting invitation: a lunch appointment in a private dining room back at HQ.

Chapter 22

Which is how I find myself in the business suite at a five star hotel on Park Lane, London. We're participating in an implementation planning meeting, creating the process to make this merger happen. It's being led by the key directors of the two businesses that will merge.

I am, though, hacked off that they have booked this five day jamboree to be held here. Don't get me wrong, it's a fabulous location, and no doubt appropriate in certain circumstances, but the conference alone, including food, will probably cost ten grand. And these guys have been holding a pre-meeting to prepare for this wider session. With business class plane tickets for the twenty or so participants from around the globe, the travel bill too must be enormous.

Heaven alone knows what is being spent. These are two loss-making businesses – what on earth are they doing renting a meeting room for twenty delegates for five days at some of the most expensive real estate on the planet? The cash that is being spent in moving this deal forward is starting to make me feel uncomfortable.

However, here we are, with a delightful view of the Park and the Queen Mother Gate. The sun is streaming in and there are racks of mineral water (both sparkling and still) on hand to keep us refreshed. The purpose of the session is to plan the implementation of the merger, so what the merged business will look like, and what will be entailed in getting to that. As members of the headquarters team, people like Tad, Arlene and I are here to spot real-time issues and either work them to satisfaction or at least trigger work on a solution. We also want to ensure that the original plans are delivered, like the form of the marriage.

Being here is all very sensible, but progress is slow, as many participants frequently aren't needed for individual points. We hook up our laptops to the suite's Wi-Fi and in the gaps quietly get on with emails and other work.

I arrived late on Sunday, as did most people. I'll be here all week, taking advantage of being in London to go meet various contacts (and in my spare time meet friends and check over my London apartment that I'm renting out whilst in Geneva). The group keeps on *breaking out* to discuss issues, so as to *gain consensus,* and it seems like this is happening for every single item. Apart from being an excruciatingly slow way to proceed, it has become apparent that nothing is really being debated by the group. Opinions are being sidelined, generalities offered, and the conclusions are well-minded but short on detail.

It is now Wednesday.

"Item 3 on the agenda" intones Mack, who is co-chairing the meeting, "Rationalisation."

There is a pause, with some slight shuffling in seats from some, and absolute stillness from others.

"As we all know, the study led by Tad concluded that the optimal approach would be to rationalize Toulouse and Milan, and concentrate production in Romania and Newcastle, with efficiency improvements in the States."

"Mack, if I may just have a moment?" This from Brett. He has a silky-smooth voice. Most people don't react, but I inadvertently look at Guillame.

This feels ominous.

"What exactly should be the basis upon which we choose to make investments in the future? For example, should we consider the impact of plans as set against cash savings? How exactly do we define what is best fit for future needs? Wouldn't it be wise to decide upon the factors that this management team wish to assess business performance, and match to those?"

So that is it. He's trying to get the group to rethink the entire process, and no doubt try to swing the choice of factors toward those that will ultimately produce the selections that our Board approved in the mysterious alternate paper. I am all for leadership of the Board, but until the mystery of just what happened to the paper is unraveled, what ought to be done?

It's a clever approach too. No-one wants to sound like a dodo, everyone wants to be perceived as wise. But it is a loaded question nevertheless – current year cash savings become paramount in terms of deciding which sites to rationalize, even though such sites could be best fit for the future, but his query effectively rules out that possibility. He is trying to unravel months of work and I can see some confused faces as folks around the table try to work out how to respond to this.

You have to admire how neat his approach is. Shifty, but neat. Time though, to head him off at the pass.

"Folks, why doesn't the team simply identify the relevant criteria and rank them? That way, the thinking will be location neutral and unbiased by work to-date by the HQ teams. It would also give the management team the opportunity to focus on a task that is of critical importance to the long term survival of the business, but without the bias that comes from their historic employments, liberating them to truly create a paradigm shift for this new business by creating a new business culture."

It's a killer response, littered with jargon, enthusiastic and all-nigh impossible to say no to. And it opens the decision process to the longer term good, just like we had originally envisaged. Brett looks annoyed, but before he can get back to me, Arlene kicks in.

"I like that idea. It builds upon the strategy and sales decisions taken so far in this meeting, ensuring that they coherently fit together."

"And our study can be used by the team to supply site and shop floor data with costed-out options and consequences." Sounds like Tad is buying in, too.

Heads nod around the table, people buy in and the group agrees to work that way.

Brett appraises the three of us coolly. The process hasn't gone the way he wanted, and we haven't heard the last from him; all that we have done is head him off, temporarily. But Guillame looks surprised to have seen the way that Tad, Arlene and I swung that outcome. He must know that this wasn't pre-planned, after all, he and I travelled in together. Have we just queered the pitch for him, for what he was planning, though?

I realize that the time has arrived to discuss the Board paper with Tad and Arlene, and my discussion with Guillame. That evening, I am hosting a supper for them: I need to discuss these events with them, sound them out about what to do. This has got to be a great chance to do so.

Chapter 23

Tad, Arlene and I have developed strong bonds over the last year or so. It isn't just the co-operative working style that we each clearly favour. We are acting as a team, for the common good, under testing circumstances. I'm on my way to my old apartment to make supper, and as the cab drives past the Royal Albert Hall in Kensington I realize that it is a real pleasure to work with them.

I've seen teams with people who will say "this is a team effort", but at the first sign of challenge jump into the nearest trench, donning a tin hat and lobbing hand grenades as they go. Throw mud, ask questions later. Those teams are rarely a team in any true sense, more a collective of increasingly stressed individuals worriedly trying to cover their backs in advance. It can become an impossible working environment, and I am lucky, I realize, to have in Arlene and Tad two people who just don't play those games.

However, this does mean that is my turn to host an evening, and with some pressure to produce a good one. I'm currently on an expat posting in Switzerland, but I've kept my apartment in London. Luckily, it had been refurbished just before the posting came up so was presentable, and for the last year or so has been rented out to a lawyer fresh from a calamitous relationship collapse. She's just found a place of her own and moved out, and in my spare time on this visit I am going over the place.

It makes sense as an arrangement. Part of me wanted to hold the dinner in Geneva, when we were next all there, but this somehow seemed the right time. Certainly, Arlene and Tad had jumped at the chance when I offered it last week.

But, I'm not married, no children, no pets, no chains, and as the evening approaches, I've become aware of the difference between the apartment (now a coldly anonymous rental space) and the warm, family-filled homes that have been the previous destinations for our suppers. Friends have offered to join the evening, to show my two work colleagues what my single family is like (which was so sweet) and I'd been tempted. But then the discussion with Guillame happened, and suddenly the evening presents itself as a great way to talk, away from the office. So that is what it is going to be: good food, good drink, good company, studiedly casual, nothing more, nothing less.

I rush into the apartment ahead of the other two, arms loaded with flowers, food and my favourite wines. Deciding what to supply has been hard work – the UK has absorbed so many food influences over the last fifteen years or so that 'British cuisine' has become a smorgasbord of exceptional flavours and twists on long-established favourites.

When planning I also knew I wouldn't have hours and hours to prepare, so had asked my fishmonger to remove the sinew in the monkfish tails ahead of time for me, ordered the wine pre-chilled and the flowers pre-arranged, and generally adopted city-dwellers' short cuts.

Despite two mad hours of preparation, it still feels like cheating, however, though my guilt trip ends when Arlene and Tad arrive. They are brimming with news.

"Teddi, you'll not believe what we saw."

"I probably won't," laughing. "Go on, what has happened?"

"We saw Guillame climbing out of a cab and heading into a house in Chelsea." They name a street of gorgeous houses just off the Embankment.

"That's a ways from Park Lane. Are you sure?"

"Sure as I'm standing here". This from Arlene. "After we saw him get out of the cab we knew we wanted to find out where we were, and we started to look at street signs. We definitely saw the signs at the next intersection, so yes, we're sure."

"Well he doesn't live in London. His family all hail from the Lake Como area, if I'm not mistaken; not sure that he has ever even lived in the UK."

We all pause in thought.

"Ah but you know, I'm sure it was innocent. I mean, he must have friends in London he visits," and I give them a knowing smile, as if to say, but hey isn't that just what you're doing.

"You don't get it. As he got out of the cab, he looked around, as if checking no-one was watching him."

"It's true, we both saw it." Fact-driven Tad. "He looked up and down the street before walking up some steps to the door of a townhouse. We saw the door number, and the guy who opened it."

"Well that is interesting, no two ways about it. Look, I wasn't going to mention this till after dinner, but there is something that you need to know about regarding Guillame."

They look at me, eye brows raised, and at each

other. Clearly, none of us is a party to all of the evenings' mysteries, not yet anyway.

"Let me just get you both a drink and set out nibbles, then I'll fill you in, " I murmur, and moments later we are comfortably housed in a couple of large Italian leather sofas, glasses of my favourite sauvignon blanc in hand.

"A couple of weeks ago, we received a copy of the Board paper and supporting documents from Armand's PA. Well, from her. Do you recall that?"

"You mean the one that she sent and tried to recall, or the other one that followed and that Brett resent a little later?"

So, straight to the point with Arlene.

"Did you get two versions, Tad, or just one?"

"Yes, I received two versions, also."

"And have either of you reviewed the contents side-by-side? Particularly the recommendations?"

They both pause. This is the last point of deniability. Suddenly, they both start to talk, excitedly, rapidly, over-talking one another (which is unlike them). A cacophony.

"Ok, ok guys. Thank heaven you both saw it, I thought I was the only one. "

They both visibly relax.

"Me too, it's been a nightmare."

"But what is going on, Teddi?"

Tad is sitting still, so still a bird-watcher would be proud. It is unlike him, he is always active, always moving. I look at Arlene – she is watching us both. Steadily.

"I have no idea. I'm in the same boat as the two of you on this. My first thought is that we weren't supposed to see the first version. "

They nod agreement. Still no movement.

"What we don't know is why the changes were

made. Could be that they know some material facts that we don't. Perhaps some very sensitive information. In which case it would be nice to know, so we can be up to speed, but at least we would then also know that the decision by the Board, and the existence of two versions, has a rational basis."

They nod again.

"It could equally be something a whole lot less wholesome. And we aren't clear whether this is Brett on his own making the changes, Brett and say Armand, or even the whole Board. Either way, in these scenarios we are into tricky waters, I would say."

Nods.

"But why would this happen? What would be the purpose of such a decision? I've been trying to figure out an answer to this, but so far nothing."

"And I, also, Teddi. Why would the Board distort the facts and outcomes away from my report?"

Tad looks miserable, Arlene hacked off. They each reach for the hors d'oeuvres, which are disappearing fast.

"Well, I have no idea, either. One thing intrigues me though. What was the reference to a PBR all about? What is that, and why would achieving one hundred percent this year matter? It clearly does, else why place it in the paper in a way that makes it seem a decisive factor? What does PBR stand for, any ideas?"

Tad shakes his head, but Arlene looks thoughtful.

"Teddi, I hadn't really focused on that so far, but you may just have hit the nail on the head."

This time it is Tad and I's turn to look taken aback. However, I'm famished, and I suspect they are, also, so before Arlene can expand upon that, I suggest we move to the table, start eating, and talk about this over the food. Gives us all time to contemplate where this conversation may be headed, too. A little later, over the pepper-crusted monkfish, Tad brings the topic of conversation back to the elephant in the room.

"That was quite a statement you made back there, Arlene. Care to explain?"

"Well, I haven't been focusing on that point in the paper, more upon the consequences of the changes made, but Teddi mentioning it suddenly put me in mind of some work we did in the States a year or two ago."

She pauses, infuriatingly, to take a bite of fish, before continuing. Talk about savouring being in the moment.

"We were looking to update the pay and benefits of the senior team, and as part of that asked external specialists in remuneration packages to come up with some ideas. We were working on how to structure the bonuses in the long term incentive plan, what we can an LTIP. These things had a target that would be set at the start of the year, and which the employees concerned would work towards during the year," she adds.

"So there we were, asking lots of questions about implementation, when one of them talked about how we would track our progress through the year as against the target set out at the start of the year. I'm trying hard to recall exactly what he said, but it was something like expressing progress as a factor of the amount of bonus that would be paid."

She pauses and looks at us.

"Could PBF be code for Paid Bonus Factor?"

There is stunned silence, as we let this

bombshell sink in. It's blatantly obvious, when you think about it. Suddenly everything starts to fall into place, and the picture isn't pretty. Surely this can't be true?

I look around the table. Conversation has stopped, eating has come to a halt, and wine glasses lie untouched.

"Well that could explain why the recommendations changed…"

Tad is looking even more miserable, and sounding increasingly cynical. Not a surprise. If correct, factories will close, research will collapse, people will lose their jobs, and all just to increase the Boards' bonuses this year.

It's mind-blowing.

Chapter 24

"Guys, I think it's high time that I explained about Guillame."

We're back on the sofas. Interest in eating has disappeared completely, so I've cleared up, escorted Tad and Arlene back to the comfy seats, and made up hot, strong coffees. Ethiopian, from the Yirgacheffe region. Awesomely aromatic, floral, lush and decadent. But, they're both looking distracted, worried and just plain miserable. I could be serving dust off the coffee warehouse floor for all the difference it is making.

"Look, this is relevant to what Arlene just said. Possibly even more so than we realize."

"Teddi, I don't think we have time for distractions right now."

"I'm with Tad on this."

"Hear me out. If it doesn't sound relevant after five minutes then cut me right off."

"Well, I suppose you normally do talk a lot of sense…OK. Let's hear it."

I take a sip of coffee.

"It's like this. I shared a car to Geneva International Airport with Guillame on Sunday afternoon. You know, on our way here? Well I asked him if he had read the emails. Turns out he hadn't at that point as he had been on vacation. He didn't even know there were two versions, let alone whether he still had both versions of the paper. I gave him a quick heads up, said that the recommendations had changed, and that I wasn't happy with the outcome. I also mentioned that one version of the Board paper, the one that the temp tried to recall, mentioned reaching 100% of PBF. He looked pretty stunned when I told him: at the time I thought that that was in relation to the recommendations, but based upon Arlene's analysis he may well have understood the reference to PBF. Anyway, upshot was that he is going to spend a couple of weeks trying to investigate this behind the scenes, see if there are, say, some material facts that we weren't aware of when putting the paper together."

They're looking at me steadily now.

"Can we trust him? Do you trust him, Teddi?"

"Good question. I mean, I didn't plan to talk with him about this. I guess it was the pressure of worrying about it for two weeks and not knowing what to do, then bumping into someone who is respected across the business but relatively to one side of the event in question. I must admit I have always liked him. He has always seemed pretty straight. What about you guys?"

"Well I would agree with your general assessment of him."

Arlene is agreeing, but Tad is shaking his head.

"It's not a case of whether we trust him. That isn't the relevant question." He pauses. "The report I prepared was thorough. I prepared it in conjunction with my counterpart from Wildcat. There is no operational reason to deviate from the conclusions. Do neither of you not understand this? That this is why I am so angry and worried right now?"

"Tad, of course we do." Arlene, bless her, is

working to calm Tad down. "Teddi, tell us a little more about the conversation with Guillame. When did he start to look upset? Did he ask any questions? How did he react throughout the conversation?"

"That's the interesting thing, Arlene. It's good that you mention it. First of all he looked stunned. We were walking into the terminal, I was talking under my breath to him, and I suddenly realized that he had actually stopped walking and was staring at me. After that he looked angry, in an icy sort of way, and then, well, something quite different…distant, thinking hard, but very focused. He asked how I had treated the attachments, and wanted to know who I had to spoken to about them."

They aren't looking entirely comfortable with this. Quizzical yes, but not entirely comfortable.

"I told him I had stored them electronically and printed copies. Funnily enough, something your wife had said came to mind when I was chatting with Guillame. You might remember the conversation we had about how difficult it is to truly delete information? You know, hitting 'delete' only places a zero in front of the information allowing it to be over-written, but doesn't actually delete it? He speculated that even if only a proportion of the email addressees had done the same, then the information would by now be pretty widely dispersed. At the time I felt comfortable about that as an outcome, and I still do. I also told him I hadn't mentioned this to anyone, but I'm not too sure he believes that part now, after the way we all headed off Brett today in the meeting. We did look pretty co-ordinated, even though as we all know we were each reacting to the situation independently."

Tad is looking a lot calmer now.

"So this could be very closely linked to our sighting of him this evening?"

"Quite possibly, though how?"

"I've just been thinking about that. Are any other Board members originally from the UK, or living here? How about the other committees like the audit committee, or the pay committee? How about the supervisory board?"

"Don't ask me, Arlene, I'm just from operations."

"But I bet we can find out. What's more, we might be able to find out who lives at that address, and match the two. I'm thinking of a Land Registry search for the latter. We can do it online."

Arlene looks impressed.

"You guys can do that here?"

"Yes, for a small fee, a few pounds, anyone with access to the internet can do it. Trouble is, the person living there may not be the legal owner, it may be rented, and it might even be owned corporately. There's no guarantee of success."

There is a pause while we all digest this. I'm pouring coffee again when Tad yawns and stretches.

"Look ladies, I am dog tired. We can't talk about this all night, but we do need a plan of action. This is my suggestion. We leave it with Guillame for now. In the meantime, we try to dig out names. We agree to talk once Teddi has heard from Guillame. I'm not sure what we can do without breaching the confidentiality agreements in out employment contracts, but at least we will know where we stand. And we don't right now."

"Agreed. Since Teddi has the job of linking with Guillame, I'll volunteer for the digging. I am very curious to see what we can unearth." Arlene steps into the breach. Again. "Just one last thought. If a property is corporately owned, can that be traced also?"

"Possibly. If it is a UK company, its accounts will be filed with Companies House as a matter of record, and again you can get those over the net for a modest fee. If it's a private company, then the shareholders should be listed, but if owned by a group, well the ultimate owner will be a lot harder to track. There has also been a trend in recent years to place substantial properties into overseas ownership, usually located in a tax or finance haven, in which case you may encounter a lot more difficulty. You might be able to trace the transaction that placed the property into the haven in the first instance, but thereafter you're looking for buyers and sellers of the shares in a company that is registered in a place that doesn't want you to know that kind of thing. Probably not easy, if not downright impossible."

"Well I'll see what I can do."

"And I'll sort out a conference call for us to follow up with. I may even be in Geneva in a couple of weeks, Teddi, so we can talk with Arlene direct from there?"

And with that we break up, and Tad and Arlene head off for a taxi back to the hotel.

We each have something to do, but as I clear up after the evening that hadn't turned out to be the jolly event I had hoped for, I can't help but feel doubts despite Arlene's reassurances and both despite and because of Tad's imprecations.

I still think the question about trusting Guillame is relevant. When I mentioned the PBF, he didn't look embarrassed, or guilty, in any way. More a degree of anger directed outwards from our conversation.

What I'm not clear about is what he can achieve, and how safe our jobs. On reflection, leveling with myself, did I mention the data security to him in the vain hope of protecting myself? Convincing him somehow that the issue couldn't be 'dry cleaned' out of the corporate record, so that somehow I couldn't either? But is this just wishful thinking, on my part? There is, as everyone knows, the spectre of redundancy, the way that criteria can be devised to ensure that a person, or category of people, is targeted: it must be legally robust, else why would it happen, though it doesn't feel morally attractive.

All in all, I'm not feeling even remotely convinced that all will be well, and it's too late to call Christoph for a spot of loving reassurance. Maybe this is just an overdose of paranoia, but I go to bed feeling more down than I have in quite some time.

Chapter 25

It's Sunday morning before I fly back to Geneva. My apartment is ready to be let again, I've caught up with a few contacts and last night met up with a couple of my closest friends, Immy and Issy, stalwarts I've known since my first days at University.

It was fab to see them again, just the best. I've missed them more than I had realized. We munched our way through sushi and drank our way through more wine than was probably sensible.

We usually stay in touch on IM, but it's weird how much better face to face time really is. I'm coming to the inescapable conclusion that social media conversations are over-hyped, that an electronic conversation is no conversation at all, when Immy suddenly asks how my love life is going.

I knew we would get onto this topic, we always do. Life is just too complex not to. Immy has been dating a barrister and got engaged a month ago, and Issy is getting married in in the next few weeks. They know I'm seeing Christoph.

"So how long's it been, Teddi?"

Teddi, not Theodora. Immy, not Imogen. Issy not Alicia. Teddi, a name of affection.

"Oh, a little over a year," I reply, airily. It's more like sixteen months, but I'm not at all sure that I want to go into this in huge detail.

Thanks, Immy.

"And you know what that means."

Thanks, Issy.

"If a guy hasn't proposed within eighteen months he never will," Immy adds, helpfully (in her view).

"Yes, I know you guys have this weird time line for love in your heads. By six months it has to be love and move to the next level. A proposal around twelve months, latest at eighteen months. Married within a year of the proposal."

I try to laugh, nonchalantly, but they're having none of it.

"It worked for me," Immy states.

"And me," adds Issy. "Teddi, it isn't about whether a guy is a bad person or not. It's just that if it's going to work, that how it turns out."

"Whether they admit it or not guys like to hunt, like to think they're dating someone other guys want to date, " interjects Immy. "They propose because they want to take that female off the market."

"And they'll only do that if you're worth it. It's about self-respect," concludes Issy. "You have to be tough, respect yourself, make your needs equal to theirs."

"Ah, you're right, as ever," I smile at them. Truth is, they probably are, certainly the part about respecting yourself and not being a doormat. Maybe it's little more than that, when all comes to all.

If I'm honest with myself, I've been wondering about Christoph and me for some time now. I love him utterly, he's my soul mate, my ever after. We make love like that, we talk like that. But, no engagement, not even a hint. It feels like it could all end today, and I'm fighting feeling down, no doubt about it.

I board the plane with these thoughts hanging heavily around my head. Maybe I'm sticking my head in the sand; one day, soon, this will all have to be confronted.

Chapter 26

"Hey, Teddi, this is Arlene."

"Arlene! Wow, lovely to hear from you. Look, did we agree to talk now? I must have messed up – I don't have it in my calendar?"

"No, you did not mess up, Teddi. Sorry to put you on the spot, but I want to update you on my research, but be as discreet as possible too. I've got Tad on the line. Are you free?"

"As luck would have it, yes. My two o'clock just cancelled."

This is odd. Arlene wouldn't normally be so pushy. Maybe this is the side of her that has enabled her to achieve what she has?

"Great, glad to hear it."

"Hey Teddi, This is Tad, pleased you can join the call."

"Thanks Tad, just glad this is how the diaries have worked out, but you guys do know that I haven't spoken with Guillame yet, don't you? That that is in two days?"

"That's why this call is so urgent, Teddi. I want you to know what I know, before you see him. Pre-warned is pre-armed, as they say."

Wow, Arlene really is wound up about something.

"OK, Arlene, shoot."

"Look guys, I'm going to jump straight in and

tell you what I found. I'll post the research materials to your home addresses after the call, if that is ok, for you to read as you see fit."

There is a rustling of papers.

"The first thing I did was check out listings for the names of people on the Board and Supervisory Board of the listed company, the non-executives, and on the audit and pay committees. All the groups we mentioned back in London."

She pauses, we don't interrupt.

"I'll send the lists through to you, but you will note that there are only three Brits in total. I tried to find out their home addresses, but two are long term residents of Geneva, been there for at least ten years, so I moved onto the third name. As far as I can work out, that individual lives outside London: I caught some golf club news that linked him to a club in the Home Counties. I don't know what the Home Counties are Teddi, maybe you could enlighten us, but it didn't sound like the term includes London?"

Again she paused. I wondered if she was sipping coffee.

"That's correct, Arlene. The Home Counties are just on the edge of London, a mixture of green fields and commuter belt. But they don't include London, so your conclusion was spot on. Now I know you, Arlene, you don't give up easily. In fact, you are one of the most tenacious people I know. That piece of research didn't produce any leads, so what did you do next?"

She laughs. "Thank you Teddi. Well, I then wondered if any of the others were living in London, even if not Brits by birth. The company website is pretty good for high-level biographical details. Nothing overtly intrusive, of course, but the sort of information that says that someone is say Swiss or French or American, or suggests they have spent their entire career in a country. It's not an exact science, but I can't find anyone who obviously fits the bill of living in London at the moment."

There's a silence.

"Hold on a minute, Arlene, you didn't get Teddi and I onto a call just to let us know that you couldn't find anything. For one thing, there's nothing that you have just said that is time sensitive. Teddi didn't need to know that before she meets with Guillame. More importantly, it's unlike you. So, why don't you tell us what you have? We both know you have something."

"That's right Arlene, quit holding back. Time to spill the beans."

"Guys, you know me so well. Well, it all starts with the other strand of research that we identified – tracing ownership of the property. I came across what Teddi had warned about; the property is owned by a trust in the Bahamas. I can't get any data on it, but in the UK records I did find the name of the guy who transferred the property into the trust, about five years back."

Another of Arlene's pauses followed. You could've cut the silence with a steak knife, hewed your way through it sinew by sinew.

"The guy who owned it back then is one Robert Finch. He's not easy to track down. He seems to head up some consultancy that advises governments."

"On what? What's his area of expertise?" asks Tad.

"Tad, I can't conclusively say. It isn't at all clear. I've noted tangential references to him, in the context of meetings between various political leaders. Once or twice in the background at briefings. Nothing concrete. But, what I did track down is that in his early years he was in finance, most recently with a bank."

Crikey. That's a turn up for the books.

"So what you're extrapolating, Arlene, and correct me if I'm misunderstanding what you have just said, is that he is some sort of adviser on banking or finance matters? Maybe a lobbyist for the banking sector?"

"That's where this looks to be heading, Teddi."

There is a stunned silence.

"So that's why you wanted us on the phone Arlene? Make sure that Teddi knew that Guillame might be in touch with a banking sector lobbyist?"

"Basically, yes. But there are some huge holes in my research, and the conclusion is full of conjecture. The guy there now *might* not be that guy, I mean the house could've changed hands. Even if it's the same guy, he may not be a pro-banking lobbyist."

"He might yet be just some social connection that Guillame was catching up with. I mean, we really haven't pinned down who he is."

"Now that isn't totally true, Teddi. Tad and I got a brief look at the guy who opened the door. I've tracked down a photo taken at a government briefing, and tucked away in the background is the same guy. For sure, there are lots of guys in the photo around, but I'm fairly comfortable it's him. Tad, maybe you can look it over when the document bundle reaches you, see if you agree?"

"More than happy to, Arlene. And a good spot, if I may say so? Can't have been easy to find?"

"Not even slightly. It was my son that gave me the lead. He found me slumped over my laptop late one evening. I'd been trawling the net, getting nowhere on a photo, when he suggested that I try some of the conspiracy sites on the internet. It was under some discussion about F.O.U.R.T.H."

Chapter 27

"4th? What's that?"

"Teddi, I had no more of an idea about that than you do right now, and I probably don't know much now." She laughs, and then continues. "Seriously, it's described as some form of secret inter-governmental back-channel on financial matters. Stands for Financial Offline Urgent goveRnmenT Horizon. Or FOURTH." She emphasizes the upper case letters. "There's a lot of speculation about what it does, and I guess whether it is even real, but there are photos and names on one site. I guess it's an attempt to weave some form of convincing story about this group, but there, tucked away in one corner of a photo, is the guy, the guy we saw open the door to Guillame that evening. Well, I *think* it's him."

"Wow, Arlene. A top-secret inter-governmental forum?"

"That's right…."

We pause, to absorb the news.

"Arlene, Teddi, what have we stumbled upon? What the hell is going on?"

Dear grief, I know just how he feels. Arlene must too; her sighs drift down the line. I decide to try and move this forward.

"O-kay. Right now, we are all wondering what is going on, and how on earth to deal with this situation, right? The way I see it, we have Guillame meeting with this special adviser. It may, or may not, be linked with the work of some secret organization, and it may, or may not, be in a banking context. It may, or may not, be linked to the changes to the Board paper. Right now, we have lot of conjecture, some of which is pretty scary, but very little in the way of concrete fact."

They pause.

"Go on, Teddi"

"Thanks Arlene. Well the way I see it, we need to think about each option, try and work out a plan or a response. That way, we can get a handle on how to move forward. Even if it is simply to resign."

I try to laugh, an attempt at brevity to lighten the situation, but it just isn't working.

"And just what do you suggest Teddi? Just how do we *'move forward'* with this?" Tad's voice oozes with sarcasm.

I take a deep breath before jumping in.

"Fair comment. Sorry. Well, let's take it all at face value. Let's assume the guy really is a member of this secret organization. Let's add in too that Guillame went to see him to discuss the Board paper, or at least the reference to what we think is Paid Bonus Factor. Why would Guillame talk to a guy like that about an internal matter? What's the motive? On the plus side, maybe the guy has some wise counsel for Guillame about how to handle it, perhaps gleaned from wider experiences. Guillame would need to be able to speak to him discreetly, behind the scenes, hence the meeting, right? Alternatively, and if we descend into the world of conspiracy theory, and perhaps give it all a paranoid twist, it's all part of a grand, global plan to protect the ability of CEO's and Boards to dictate ever more exorbitant pay packages irrespective of business performance."

"There could be other motives too, but your point is well made. We need to understand Guillame's motive for the meeting, what he hoped to achieve from it, and whether he did achieve anything. I mean, we're assuming that there was an outcome. There may have been nothing of the sort."

"Well put, Tad, nailed it in one."

"Guys, I have to say I concur, but Teddi, I don't agree with the point about exorbitant pay packages for CEOs and Boards. I don't agree that CEO pay *is* exorbitant."

"You don't, Arlene?"

"Not at all. A business has to pay the going rate for its people, whether they are in assembly on the shop floor, or on the Board making the big decisions. These things are carefully thought through and benchmarked to information about competitors. How can you say that this is exorbitant? This is the market rate."

"Ah, Arlene, you know, I don't disagree with you about the general process? I don't even disagree with you about following the market. But the question here is, just what *is* the market? External consultants in head hunter firms and banks provide reports on general pay levels. So, and for example, if a CEO's performance is spot on, he or she will point to these reports and demand an increase. "If I am a top performer, you must pay me as such" he or she will say, and he or she will point to the better pay deals in the report. Crikey, he or she may even wander in with another business's public accounts, point to the pay section, and demand the same for himself. But the snag is, this is the self-same information that the consultants and banks will provide to all the others. They just keep on updating it for each pay deal. So it's a self-fulfilling upward spiral that is utterly unchecked and uncheckable, by its very nature."

"Teddi, you can't believe that, surely? That is just anti-business, anti-capitalist."

"Arlene, criticizing Board pay isn't anti-business. It isn't anti-capitalist. If anything, it is direct proof that capitalism is strong and well and thriving."

I pause. No feedback.

"OK, guys, look I can see that you're finding my statements to be challenging, and after Arlene's bombshell no-one is in the mood for controversy. I can see I'd better explain how I'm seeing this."

There is a terse silence. None of the usual friendly stuff like 'ok' or 'go ahead.'

"The way I see it, capitalism is simply a buy-sell arrangement. Nothing more, but also nothing less. If willing buyers and sellers can be found, a market will come into being. It's an amazingly vibrant interaction, and has generated some of society's most significant leaps. For example, the Gutenberg bible was printed to allow people to understand the Bible for themselves, basically giving them a fundamental freedom of interpretation and self-determination. The buy-sell has given us brilliant engineers to work for a salary and create some of the most stunning innovations that mankind has ever known. The simple buy-sell is amazing, and a fundamental part of our lives. But, and this is a big but, it can lead to some very unwise outcomes. Think about it. The buy-sell has sent children up chimneys and onto factory floors. It has sent them into prostitution, and worse. It has sold people based on the colour of their skin to supply cotton plantations with cheap labour. Things that we absolutely abhor have happened when supply has met demand. Even forcing and oppressing people in the process, destroying their lives. No, CEO pay is not in the same category of pain as these terrible practices. What we have learned, though, one of the things that these awful events throughout history have taught us, is that the buy-sell is not a moral force. It can lead to terrible and tragic outcomes, and that man, as a moral being, has to be on its guard to identify these as they arise and curtail them."

I pause to take a sip of water, and collect my thoughts if I am honest with myself.

"And your argument is that the pay of senior executives, the Board, is one of these?"

Chapter 28

Tad has added this very quietly.

"Tad, something like that. We know the role of the Board is to make money for the shareholders. In most big businesses those shareholders are you and I, through our pension plans, our 401(k) plans, and our investments. We don't have much say, day to day, so the non-Executives are tasked to manage this for us. But problems kick in. The non-Execs start to rely on outside advisers. Maybe they see the same thing in other businesses. Heck, their pay is determined in the same way. We end up with a situation where the average CEO's salary rockets from say six hundred thousand in 2000 to four million by 2012, as the spiral ratchets ever higher and ever faster. The real work barely changes over that time. The shareholders are the ones that lose. It's this loss to the shareholders that is anti-business."

"So you're saying that it's an extreme version of the buy-sell? Kind of one of the moral aberrations that happen, that we have to change, in order to actually *do* business?"

"Mmmn, Arlene. That's pretty much it."

"But what about the individuals themselves? Are we saying that they are morally repugnant in some way? I'm not sure that I could agree with that, Teddi, not sure that I could go along with that at all. To me it's all about motivation. If you tell a guy he will get paid, or more pay, by doing something, then surely that is exactly what he will pursue? If we assume people behave rationally in their best interests."

It's a good point, and I tell her so.

"Can't agree more, Arlene. If you think about it, the entire value system that seems to be created rests on money. How much you earn, how much more you can earn, and what you have to do to achieve that. Failure can cost you money, even down to costing you your job and hence ability to get money."

"So let me get this right. The logical extension of that argument is that a Board will take decisions that aren't necessarily in the long-term interest of a business, but rather for some short-term response?"

"I guess so, Tad, if the big investors say that's what they want, and the Boards' bonuses are structured that way…."

We pause, collectively. This isn't quite where I expected this conversation to head, and I'm guessing that they're looking at this in the same way. It's Tad who picks up the gauntlet again.

"But what is the solution, Teddi? Central pay control? Morals by political fiat? Teddi, you must surely know that the alternative to capitalism isn't viable. I come from a country that has lived through the alternative, and it can never again be envisaged."

"I'm behind you on that one." Arlene echoes Tad.

"Guys, I don't disagree with you. The day we can rely on and trust our political masters provide reliable, consistent, moral-based guidance is a day that will probably never come."

I pause, again.

"Actually, strike that. It may well be the case, but we can't allow ourselves to sink into cynical despondency."

"Which would be easy here," Tad interjects.

"Agreed, which would be easy here, so let's get this back on track. The way I see it, the current practice treats members of the Board as if they are somehow so utterly amazing that the business would be mad to let them go. If you take that analogy to the extreme, then when the current crop dies out or retires, so say in twenty years or so, tops, the entire, global business community will face cataclysm, as there will be no more of them. Which is self-evidently claptrap. Given that it is utter nonsense, what can we therefore conclude about the original presumption?

Members of a Board just don't magically appear out of thin air. They aren't somehow brought into being just at that moment of accepting appointment. The brutal reality is that these people all have a career history. They have all climbed the ranks. They have all been nothing before being something. What you can probably say is that they have understood how to make that climb and done so, but what you can also say is that there are plenty more where they came from. It's the very nature of the beast.

My guess is that, if you were to retire every single Board member, in one fell swoop, you would be able to replace them with people below them in the organization. Not only that, you could do so at a lower salary. People are hungry, that hunger is there, and there will always be people who will take a job, at a lower salary than the other candidate, if it's the deciding factor. It's that buy-sell thing again."

"So what you're saying, if I'm hearing you right, is that our business replaces the Board?"

Chapter 29

Tad sounds a little taken aback.

"I think we are looking at two separate issues. I mean, ok they're related, by they're still separate. One is the general issue of executive pay, the other how we respond to what happened to the Board paper, based on everything we know so far."

I pause to sip water, and keep my brain rehydrated. There are times when it feels like I am leaping from mountain top to mountain top to draw something together, and this is one of them. I rub my temples.

"Sorry about the pause guys. Just sipping water. Feel like I am talking way too much."

Arlene laughs, gently. "It's ok, Teddi. If I am brutally honest with you here, I am enjoying this conversation. It's good to revisit old assumptions. Sometimes you can be so wrapped up inside a situation, you can no longer step back from it. It feels like we are looking at this from a very different perspective, with distance, and I have to say I'm learning a lot from it. And I like learning."

"Thanks Arlene. Right, the big issue first - let's get that out of the way. This is an issue affecting a small group in each business. I know for a fact that the hiring salary for my job hasn't changed since the year 2000. You can go out and hire someone now to do this job and offer the exact same salary that you would have offered back then. I don't know whether the price has gone up and then shrunk back, or simply never changed, but that is the basic scenario. "

"In the spirit of openness, I would say that the same is true about my role," Tad interjects.

"And I would too," Arlene adds. Then we all laugh, a kind of collective, shared, slightly embarrassed laugh.

"So, somewhere, in an organization, there is a cut-off point, a point before which salaries have barely changed, and beyond which they are spiraling madly upward. It's that small group who exist beyond the cut-off point that should be the focus of any change. There is some published research on the issue, I'll dig out an internet link to the report I read and forward it to you, but, in essence, the rabid increases have been largely over the last ten years or so. I think it's possible to roll back the years on executive pay, and I bet you could rebase it back to about the year 2000. And cut out the whole bonus culture at the same time."

"Ok, ok, Teddi, let's say that we have a conclusion point there. Some very adventurous thinking, but let's leave it at that for now. We aren't going to change the world in one phone call. What are your thoughts on the specific issue we are dealing with? Is your thinking similarly adventurous?"

We all laugh together. Again.

"You're right, Tad, this does feel like I'm leaping from mountain top to mountain top. The reason that we latched onto this whole issue in the first place was that someone changed the Board paper: positions have been advocated, and decided upon, that we didn't sign up for or sign off on, but our names are associated with the paper. We aren't involved in the Board's decision-making processes in any way, so, and simply put, we're feeling used, and a bit threatened. We need to understand the context.

So, the first scenario we could be looking at is that time will prove that there *is* something that we didn't know of, and that this *is* nothing whatsoever to do with bonuses, after all; in that case, we could probably get to a comfort position, but we do need to know the rationale for the change. I'd also say that we ought to have known about that ahead of paper being submitted too, not after the fact.

The second scenario is at the completely opposite end of the spectrum. Let's say that the changes have been made because the result will ensure a better bonus payout for the Board, and let's say they are all in on the change. Their remuneration plan has been signed off on by shareholders. In which case, they may well argue that they have been doing what their shareholders instructed them to do. The three of us may not like the situation, but it's how it is. I guess, then, that we each have to look to our own consciences. Maybe leave the business and join another? I mean, there *are* different options, but that would probably be the end game.

"Then, there are scenarios that fit somewhere between the two. Maybe the changes were made by Brett and Armand, and the rest of the Board have no idea what has gone on. Would they prefer to know, and how would they react if they knew? Would they go along with it anyway, or would they be up in arms? There is at least one scenario that sees the rest of the Board, or some significant part, rebelling against what has happened, and in which case would we feel less threatened?"

"I guess there would need to be some form of

change though? Some removal of personnel? Maybe the end to that bonus scheme?" Tad adds this quietly, as if musing aloud. "Would we be removed also, rather than be an awkward reminder of a senior level mistake?"

"Well I'd hope not" Arlene interjects. "Teddi is right, we need to keep the really cynical interpretations at bay. It won't help our thinking at all and it will destroy our motivation. Maybe the Board will react as we have, or maybe they will go along with the changes. Either way, it will give us our lead – if they go along with the changes then we have the end game, as Teddi described, and if they react, then we maybe have a wider range of choices as employees. "

"Either way, I'm going to start putting feelers out about jobs elsewhere. I don't want this to rebound and for me to find myself "counseled out", unemployed, in an economic climate that just doesn't lend itself to an easy job hunt right now. There are tough times out there."

Tad is right. I'm thinking of Em's sister in law, Katie, or my own role back in the UK now filled by someone else, how easy it would be to replace me with a Swiss local, and leave me with nowhere to go. Not so different from Katie. Right now you can be as talented as they come, but you're still one CV out of two hundred applicants, and that is tough going by anyone's standards.

"Tad, I don't disagree with you. It's probably a wise move. Not the move any of us envisaged when we started working on the transaction. If I'm honest I thought it would be good for my CV," and I laugh ruefully.

"Me too."

"Me three," Arlene adds.

"I guess there is only one issue left on the table,

then," Tad replies, "and that is Teddi's meeting with Guillame. What will Guillame say when he sees Teddi? Will he admit to meeting this guy? What will we learn?"

"So, what questions should Teddi ask?"

"Thanks Arlene, that was running through my mind also," I add. "What are the key questions or issues we want an answer to? As a strawman, I thought we want to know the reason for the change, and whether the entire Board was in on the act, or just a small group. Either way, we need to know whether the Board is going to revisit their decision, and then we need to reflect on our response to all of that. I mention FOURTH if need be. I can mention your names if asked. How does that sound?"

"It sounds a decent run through but, Teddi, how do you feel about doing this, about having this meeting with Guillame on your own. It all sounds very unattributable. Don't you feel exposed?"

As ever, Arlene hits the nail right on the head: in truth I am feeling more terrified by the minute, this is stressing the wotsits out of me. Strangely enough, though, at the same time, deep down in the core of my being, I feel strong and calm. To be true to me, I have to get to the bottom of this issue, and I have to find an outcome that I can live with morally. But, yes, she's right. Again. And I tell her so.

"You mean isn't this all a bit David versus Goliath? Oh absolutely, Arlene. But at the same time, there is a part of me that needs to get to the bottom of this, and find a resolution that I can live with. I can understand a discussion about factory rationalization when there is oversupply, perhaps collapsing demand, but there are people's jobs on the line, livelihoods of families and communities, even the economic decline of a country, and if my name is being associated with that decision then I have to see how and why the decision is made, and I have to agree. If I don't….." and I let it trail on the wind.

"Then we might as well get the hell out of Dodge" adds Tad, and not for the first time I am grateful that these two people are on board. He said "we."

I take a deep breath, and can hear Arlene and Tad do the same.

"OK guys, I think we've concluded on what we can today. What do you think, Arlene, you called the meeting?"

"Agreed Teddi. I'm feeling comfortable that you both know the results of my research, and what our aims are for the meeting with Guillame."

"Seconded Arlene." This from Tad.

"Well, I think that that wraps it all up. I'm aiming to place a call to you both after the Thursday. If you could both ping me your availability for a couple of hours on Friday afternoon, I'd be grateful."

And with that we all make our farewells and sign off.

Chapter 30

There are times in your life when life itself tests you, measures you against some barometer of personal capability, sending you along the next twist in your journey and deciding the rest of your existence on this planet.

These moments are fleeting, often not noticed or understood until after the fact. They're the ones that you regret twenty years later, punishing yourself for the mistakes of your teenage self, or even the day after some meeting, when you realize your work chum never was and has just comprehensively shafted you, stealing your idea, presenting it as their own, and co-opting you to work for them in its execution.

They're the events that happened before, hamstring you now, and stop you making the best of tomorrow, but they are also the ones where you leap magnificently up a waterfall, like a salmon beating a bear and the current, that buoy you up and carry your trajectory upward and forward, and I have a funny feeling, deep in my bones, that my lunch with Guillame, however it plays out, is going to be one of those such moments. It feels like the next stages in my life are going to be determined over lunch.

I've put down the phone, but am struggling to settle down to work again. In front of me is a share sale agreement that needs review, but each time I look at the pages on my desk, my mind drifts away, turning over the call that just happened, and musing on the lunch yet to come. This isn't good. This job can't afford this kind of unproductive behavior, so to make matters worse I beat myself up for this, and end the day badly bent out of shape. Confused, worried, guilty, distracted.

As if that wasn't enough, Em calls by my office, just before I leave. This is how we met, her appearing in the open door of my office, looking for help in getting a powerpoint presentation together in double quick time for the Group Controller, and we often drift by one another's' door during the day, inveigling the other to wander off for a quick coffee, ostensibly to discuss some business issue or other, but also just to keep in touch.

"You got a moment, Teddi?"

"Sure, let me clear my desk and we can head off, maybe get a glass of wine somewhere? Bit late for coffee?"

"To be honest I don't have time for either right now. But something has happened and I want you to be the first to know."

This is a turn up for the books; over the year or so we have known one another she has never done this.

"Sounds intriguing. Take a pew and spill the beans old girl."

She would normally smile when I turn on the 'English-isms;' we've spent hours over the last year with me teaching her odd words and phrases, but today I don't even raise a glimmer of a smile. This is doubly odd.

"Well, I might as well get straight to the point. They're turning my role into one occupied by local staff, and sending me back to the Netherlands. I'll be back there within the month."

She looks straight at me as she says this. She's trying to look coolly remote and detached about this, but her eyes are anything but cool. Hugely furious would be a more accurate description.

I close my mouth (my jaw is on my chest).

"But that doesn't make sense. You're bringing knowledge not locally available. You've barely been here a year and a half, and your business case stated that you would need three years to effect full transfer and train up a replacement. What on earth is going on?"

"No idea Teddi. That's partly why I can't talk for long now. I'm sitting down with Human Resources in ten minutes to start a search for a replacement."

"And what will you do back in the Netherlands? Your old role is filled."

"Oh, apparently there is capacity for someone with my skills in Team 2. I was Team 1, remember?"

We look at each other. Her eyes are red rimmed, but to her credit she is holding back. We both know what this means. She's being sent back early, with no promotion, to the less regarded team. She has been doing a brilliant job here, really delivering well, but that won't mean a hill of beans when she gets home. She might as well have EPIC FAIL stamped on her forehead for all the difference it will make with her colleagues back there.

And it begs the question, who has she offended? Because someone, somewhere, is keen to get her out of the way. And has managed it.

"We need to get together, you do know that? This will take more than ten minutes to fully discuss?"

"Yes, I do. Maybe later in the week?"

We agree on Friday, after work, and she slopes off. I watch her walk down the corridor. She is normally so full of energy, but now her shoulders slope; someone in need of moral support, for sure.

I head for supper at Christoph's'. Normally, the moment we meet he smiles, butterflies leap up in my tummy and we melt together. Today, though, is different. I'm having to do it rather than it happening naturally. It's not necessarily a problem. One of those glimpses of the future, when you show a courtesy to someone you love by doing something for them, that they appreciate, even when you are knackered and grumpy and just not in the mood.

We head straight for the refrigerator and he pours out a glass of wine. I've drained mine and topped it up before realizing that he is looking at me and hasn't touched his yet.

"Bad day?"

"You have no idea."

"Try me." He takes my hand and leads me to the sofa, taking my jacket and kicking off his shoes. I get the hint: he wants me to relax too. "So tell me all about it."

"Well let's see. How about the following? I've got work coming out of my ears, my best female friend here is being sent back to the Netherlands within the month, my job looks about a safe as a mud hut in a tsunami, I've got the political lunch from hell in two days and oh, my boyfriend, whom I've been seeing for nearly a year and a half, shows no sign of wanting to move things to the next level. Whichever way I look, everything is up in the air, nothing is certain and as likely as not I'll be back in the UK myself in the next month or two and back to square one romantically. How about that, that enough for you?"

I see him flinch; he looks hurt.

"I was going to make supper but let's head out. You're in serious need of some cheering up. We need Italian food, and we know just the place. We'll be there in half an hour."

He's putting on his shoes again, but I haven't moved.

"I'm sorry."

"I know you are. This isn't you."

"But I've just said some horrible things."

He looks at me. I feel comprehended. Understood. He does, too.

"I really am sorry. Whatever I want to say, I should have found a nicer way than the way I just used."

He looks at me again.

"Yes, you should. I'm not happy about what you've just done, but there is clearly more going on than meets the eye. I think it's time you leveled with me about all this work nonsense, because whatever it is, it's tearing you apart, and you're letting it."

I nod, suddenly unable to speak.

"Come on. We've got a half hour walk in the summer, early evening sunshine when we can talk this through. How about it?"

"Sounds perfect," I manage, through tears that are suddenly welling up and threatening to overwhelm me.

So as we walk along the warm evening streets, gazing idly in windows from time to time, and heading towards our favourite Italian café, I tell Christoph everything. Literally, everything. About the Board paper that was changed, and about my calls and meetings with Arlene and Tad. About the supposed circumstances of Guillame's meeting with a member of FOURTH, and about FOURTH, whatever it is, and what we know so far. About the imminent lunch and where it could head. About Katie's fruitless, depressing hunt for a job and the reality of "merger synergies." About Em leaving, and about feeling sad at losing my friend. About the endless merry-go-round of the expat, NGO world, with the one constancy of arrivals and departures, and about not wanting to start again. About Christoph, wondering if it is going anywhere, or whether this means that he and I would be ending too.

It was about uncertainty, really, in all of its forms. Uncertainty and endings, too much uncertainty and too many endings going on at one time.

Christoph listens. Occasionally he prompts me with a small question, and occasionally he distracts me with chat about what we can see in a shop window.

Just before we get to the restaurant, he pulls me to him.

"How are you feeling about all of this, Teddi?"

"Do you know what? Until this moment I haven't been willing to admit how much it has been getting on top of me. I feel relieved to finally be discussing it with someone I can trust implicitly."

He looks at me. We both realize what this means. I don't really want things to end with Christoph – he's my best friend as well as the love of my life.

"I can see that. Over the last half hour your shoulders have lost their rounding and you've got your spring back in your step. But Teddi, this has been far too great a burden for you to carry alone.

You aren't some kind of superhero invested with strength beyond mere mortals. You're a human being who has been putting herself under immense pressure - whatever were you thinking? If we are to be together you have to trust me. I'm here for you."

He looks at me as he says this, his eyes warm, soft and enveloping. Almost apologetic. The windows onto his soul. Maybe he's wondering if he hasn't been there for me?

"Yes, I do, and yes you are," I nod. "I'll trust you. I do right now. I was just scared of mentioning the whole work issue due to confidentiality. Wish I'd talked to you earlier, feels so much better" I half smile.

"Well, I'll start to think of ideas for your lunch on Thursday, but right now we deserve salmon risotto," and with that he drags me into the restaurant.

Chapter 31

So the day dawns. Time, as is its habit, has ticked on by and the lunch drawn near. Alcohol and a large plate of risotto had helped me sleep on the Tuesday evening (that and Christoph), but Wednesday dragged. I faffed around during the morning in the office, ate too much at lunchtime including a pastry, took a few calls in the afternoon, and paced to IT to sort out a problem with my laptop. In the evening, Christoph coached me to handle the building stress: we went for a run then meditated. It didn't stop me waking at 3.30am, my mind clattering at full speed through variants of the impending conversation, but it did enable me to calm my mind again and eventually get back to sleep by 5am (though I really didn't want to hear the alarm clock an hour later).

One of Christoph's key suggestions was to find something on my To Do List to complete on the Thursday morning that would be active, that I wouldn't be able to put off, but that wouldn't up my already-high cortisol levels. I booked a two hour meeting with a project manager to run through the intricacies of a project we needed to set up, and find the time slipping by, 'though with perhaps too many cups of coffee for company.

Suddenly, it is gone twelve, and I am meeting Guillame in only a little over twenty minutes.

Barely time to dolly myself up and get to the dining room on time. Perfect. With my teeth cleaned, hair brushed, make up reapplied and drenching in my favourite perfume, I waft along the corridors and into the elevator as casually and elegantly as I can (with my stomach in knots and on new four inch heels). I look good, though, and that smidgen of confidence boost helps me settle, that and Guillame's welcoming smile.

"Teddi, lovely to see you, glad you can make it."

"Oh it's my pleasure, Guillame, great to see you too. Thank you for the invitation."

We shake hands, and then he leans in for a double air kiss. Woo, I must be a confidante, I think. That and that he is already here, waiting for me to arrive. Which strikes me as a little unusual.

Hmmn.

We stand in front of the picture window, admiring the view and making small talk whilst the waiter pours our drinks (mineral water for both of us). The waiter leaves.

"So how have you been, Teddi?"

"Just great. Busy, as you can imagine. Work pouring out of my ears and barely a moment to myself, what with all of the deal work going on at the moment."

He looks at me, raises an eyebrow gently and smiles.

"Keeping yourself busy as a distraction from this business of the Board paper? That is much to be admired, Teddi, though personally, in your shoes I would have found the wait since we last spoke to be more than a little unnerving."

He smiles, and as he does so his eyes smile with him. He's trying to open me up on this topic, gauge my perspective, but I don't feel threatened.

Either he is excellent at putting on a mask, or this is genuine. I don't know him well enough to know which is true, but my gut is telling me he can be trusted.

"Well, I can't say that I haven't thought about it at all," I reply. "And you won't have expected me to ignore it, either. But, I did agree to withhold judgement whilst you could see what you could find out, and I stand by that."

"But no concern?"

"Nothing that a run couldn't take care of."

He laughs. "Doesn't it just? I run before breakfast, how about you?"

"Really? Me too. I love the way that my body wakes up and really grabs hold of the day ahead. That and the empty streets and the cool air that clear out my mind."

"Feels like you can be alone with your thoughts. Just you and the road, and no distractions."

"Something like that," I agree. "Personal space. Very zen."

We move to the table. I'm feeling remarkably calm. It occurs to me that he is making a huge effort to get alongside me. Which could be disconcerting, given his seniority; guess the stories of his diplomacy and charm must be true.

The answer as to "why?" is still open, though.

We are tucking into gravad lax before he finally twists the conversation back onto the topic that has brought us together.

"Teddi, I have to thank you for your forbearance in the matter of the Board paper," he opens.

I nod in reply, as if to say "You're welcome," but saying nothing in reality. This is very delicate, and I realise he needs to lead the conversation for now.

"Yes, I had a lot of questions that needed

answers, queries to make as it were. It hasn't been a straightforward exercise, and I appreciate that there have been no distractions to make that harder still."

He smiles and digests more salmon, and a morsel of rye bread.

"My first query was whether I had both emails, and therefore both papers. As you noted, the Secretary to the Board sends the papers to the various Heads of Department as well as the team members. You were lucky to get both, and that the temp didn't read through them first. You may simply never have known about the change. As it was, as both head of my Department and a team member I too had received both emails, and as you had already alerted me to the possibility of change, I made sure that I opened the earliest first so that it couldn't be automatically recalled.

After that, I undertook a thorough, line-by-line review of both papers to ascertain precisely all of the changes." He paused to look at me. "Your summary at the airport barely scratched the surface."

"I'm sorry. There wasn't much time to give you all of the detail. Just the gist."

"Of course. I remember our conversation well, and that is precisely what you did."

More food. I join in; this is clearly going to take some time.

"Having established that it was changed, and what the changes were, I next resolved to discover who in the Board room that day could have been aware of the original operational data and conclusions, other than Brett. I ascertained, from the head of Tad's department, that he had sent Tad's report to Armand, and the Chief Operating Officer. No-one else, not the Head of Human

Resources, nor Finance, nor Technical. Not the Chairman, and none of the other non-execs. Not the Head of the Pay Committee, nor the Audit Committee. A very limited circulation, Brett, Armand and the COO."

I perk up, shocked. Suddenly this looks a whole lot more sinister.

Chapter 32

We pause while the plates are cleared away, and the main course arrives. Dover sole, my favourite. I am in food heaven.

"Of course, this suggested who could have known that the paper had been changed (assuming that no-one forwarded this onto any of the others). However, it was not clear, up front, whether the changes were ones that the Board would have wanted anyway. The reason for the change was still open, in my mind."

He pauses whilst we admire the sole, and tuck into the creamy, soft flesh. I'm nodding encouragingly as he speaks. Enough to encourage, but not so as I look like a car toy.

"My next step was to try to establish whether there were any decision-making criteria in operation at the Board. I used some subterfuge, I must admit: I pretended that there was a significant technical issue coming along and I needed to be fully appraised before I recommended solutions. Not necessarily incorrect, when you think about it," he smiles, slightly.

"Anyway, I met with the Global Managing Director for all three of our operating businesses and the Global Head of Legal, separately of course, asking to pick their brains, take them into my confidence as it were. They could think of nothing, no 'hidden' agenda, no operational criteria that weren't clear from the global business plan.

I was very particular. The Head of Legal asked me why I was checking like this, when the protocol for a Board paper meant that it would be reviewed, before submission, by all Heads anyway. I said that I wanted to be sure that I wasn't going to make a recommendation that would lead us to breach some agreement or commitment, that would be just pointless. I played the schmuck slightly. He bought into that, looking for informal comment or even sign off ahead of formal submission is quite normal.

So, by this point, I didn't have an established reason, but I had one ace up my sleeve."

"Paid Bonus Factor," I interject. "PBF."

He looks momentarily non-plussed, then he smiles.

"Of course, the airport. I wondered whether you had noticed that."

"Must admit at first I just noticed that you looked unhappy, and I thought that maybe that was due to the changes. But, on reflection, I realized that the real trigger was when I spoke the three letters PBF, and that set me thinking."

"I suppose I couldn't have expected anything less from you, Teddi. Ah well, now we get to the most difficult part."

He pauses, again to digest food, and I join in. As much to reassure, because by now I'm not totally sure whether I am hungry anymore.

"Teddi, are you familiar with LTIPs? Long Term Incentive Plans? They are much used, at the executive level, to provide extra incentive for the Board to perform. Part of a market-based package."

"Ah, the market-base. Yes, I've heard of LTIPs, they're often in the news these days when some executive or other finds their pay rejected by the shareholders. I've never seen the detail of one, though."

He looks at me, quizzically. Not a surprise, after all I've just implicitly criticised Board pay.

"Some eighteen months ago, we at the senior management level evaluated whether to implement an LTIP that would include the entire executive. We took guidance from experts in the compensation industry, and benchmarked pay levels, terms and so on. The experts highlighted the sheer range of options open to us in constructing the LTIP. For example, bonuses could have been paid on rises in our share price, on rises in asset prices, on costs cut, or cash hoarded. Even against stock market indices such as the FTSE 100, Fortune 500, CAC, Dax. There really was a lot of flexibility.

However, there were two general concerns with this across senior management. The first was that, in absolute terms, our pay packages have increased tremendously over the last few years, and there was some concern that we were already well paid, perceptibly so. The other concerned the construction of the LTIP itself. It was as if bonuses would be payable for performance that was surely already within the remit of our roles. It was as if increasing the share price, or saving cash, etc. etc., were somehow in addition to our day-to-day existence. Which of course then begged the question as to why were we being paid so much in our main packages: surely to have both would be double counting? I don't mind telling you, Teddi, that there was a significant level of discomfort around these issues, amongst senior management.

It felt as if we were being invited to dip our hands into the pot twice for the same thing. Not everyone agreed about the conclusion, but in certain circles it was felt to cause a certain embarrassment.

Anyway, after much review, discussion and debate we took a vote and decided not to implement the LTIP. I thought nothing more of this until that conversation between you and I at the airport."

"When you suddenly realized that the LTIP had in fact been implemented, albeit with a smaller group of participants? That must have come as quite a shock?"

"You have no idea, Teddi, truly. So my next challenge was to ascertain which individuals were included in this LTIP, and the terms."

"That can't have been easy."

"It wasn't. I didn't want to alert the audit committee chair yet, as I didn't have all of the facts, and I felt I couldn't approach the chair of the remuneration committee, who must surely have been involved in this."

"So who did you approach?"

Boy, he is stringing this out. Clearly knows how to maintain dramatic tension. Either that or so involved he has no concept of impact on Yours Truly. At that point the waiter appears to clear our plates, so he waits until coffee is served before continuing.

"The Board, as you may know, comprises the Chief Executive Officer (Armand), the Finance Director, the Chief Operating Officer, and the Heads of four technical departments – legal, technical know-how, human resources and strategic development. There are three operating businesses that report into the Chief Operating Officer, and the Managing Director of each of these is also on the Board.

Of course there are also lots of informal, dotted-line relationships. Take tax for instance: you are part of tax, which is part of finance, but you are also part of the strategic development team. The LTIP as evaluated would have incorporated the Board and the direct reports under the Board, as well as the Heads of the Remuneration and Audit Committees, and the Chairman himself. So, as an example, the Head of Tax would have been included (that is Hans, as he reports to the Finance Director), and me, as a direct report of the Head of Technical Know-How."

"And you had to find someone you could now approach. It was likely to be someone who was still included in the LTIP, but you didn't want someone who had received the original report from Tad, nor someone who had advocated the changed paper. You didn't want to trigger an external crisis until you knew the facts, and you wanted to avoid anyone with a reason to withhold the information from you. Crikey. How did you manage that?"

He smiles again, but his eyes are serious, comprehending.

"As ever, you grasp where I am heading. Tell me Teddi, in my shoes, who would you approach?"

Quite some question.

"At a guess, I would say the Chairman, the Finance Director, or maybe one of the Managing Directors. I don't know any of them, at all. What are their relationships with Armand and each other like? Where is the patronage? Any conflicts? Guess I'd like to ascertain that first. My gut is to approach the Chairman – his job is to control Armand, and if trouble is brewing he is the one who should know. But, once he knows, there is no going back. So, I'd plump for the Finance Director or one of the MDs for the initial data request, or maybe one of the folks you had already talked with, and then maybe follow that up with a meeting with the Chairman."

"Which is what I did, and it was around about the eleventh hole I think it was before our Finance Director got to the detail of the Board discussion, or at least enough for me to turn supposition into facts. The next stage was the most difficult of all, though.

I realized that people would talk about my queries, for example our Finance Director was bound to mention the golf conversation with the COO or Armand fairly soon thereafter. I knew I would have to move quickly, so met with the Chairman, and the Head of the Audit Committee, to brief them."

He paused, again.

"And, what came of that?"

To which he replied, "Tell me, Teddi, do you have an appointment immediately after lunch? Have you time for a stroll? The Jardin des Anglais looks so inviting at the moment."

Chapter 32

It hits me like a sledge hammer - we aren't going to get to the meat until we are utterly out of earshot of anyone, no risks being taken, not even potential ones. All very deniable, just like Arlene said it would be.

We wander casually out of the building and onto the Quai de Mont Blanc, looking as if for all the world we are just two colleagues out for a post-prandial leg-stretch. It is relatively empty, we can manage to limit the conversation as we pass the occasional tourist, and the breeze blows away the rest.

The warm June sun beats down on our faces. Guillame pulls out his sunglasses and immediately adopts that slightly uber-chic, north-Italian-male look. Unmistakable.

"There are going to be changes, Teddi. Substantial ones. I can't give you details as yet, as they aren't announced to the stock market, and there are very delicate and dangerous times between now and then, but there are going to be changes."

Pants. No meat after all. I must look disappointed and endeavor to hide behind my own sunglasses too, but he spots this.

"Teddi, I need you to trust me like you have never trusted me before. I really cannot tell you anything more now, but I promise, once the announcements are made, I'll call you and fill you in, answer any questions that you may have. This I promise.

Now it's my turn. I've told you what I have been up to in the context of this paper since we last spoke, how about you tell me what you have been up to? We both know that that planet brain of yours hasn't been idle all of this time."

He sees my surprise at this. "Yes Teddi, your planet brain. It may surprise you to know it, and I suspect that you don't realize it, but you are one of the most intelligent people that I have ever met. I want your take on all of this. Let's start with the market-rate – I noted your slight disgust when I mentioned that, over lunch."

I guess he is right. He has been very open about what he has been up to, and it's up to me to reciprocate. And, after all, it is what Tad, Arlene and I expected.

"Well let's start at the beginning, shall we?" I suggest.

"When you and I talked at the airport, I hadn't mentioned this to anyone. During the meeting at the hotel, Tad, Arlene and I found ourselves sharing supper one evening, and, quite by chance, we realized that we had all received and opened both copies of the email."

"I thought so. That three-way ambush laid on for Brett did give you away. Quite skillful, I thought."

"Ha, not really Guillame. I would love to be able to claim credit for Machiavellian behavior, but there was no pre-meditated ambush. We hadn't talked at that point," I quickly reply.

He looks sideways at me, as we stroll, lifting his glasses just to make eye contact. The look is querying. Not disbelieving, but not accepting either.

"When Brett started to talk about the basis for a decision, it suddenly occurred to me that he might be trying to implement the revised paper, and that this might be how. I decided to challenge him, but what struck me there and then was how quickly Tad and Arlene chimed in, in my support."

"Yes, I noted that," Guillame chips in.

"So over dinner I decided to broach the subject of the paper."

"You instigated that?"

Crap, I realise too late the trap I have just fallen into. Time to try and haul myself back out.

"Well, given how they responded, it struck me that there were at least four people around that table, excluding Brett, who knew about the change. Who's to say they wouldn't have said anything if I hadn't? In fact, I can probably claim some credit for the silence from them over the last ten days or so."

I let this sink in, and then continue, to try and press home any advantage I may have created.

"We rapidly realized that we all knew about the changes, and we were all unhappy about them. Significantly so. We discussed various issues and ways forward, and as part of that I apprised them of my discussion with you. We realized that we may not have all the relevant facts, and decided to let you continue your investigation so see what you could unearth, before we undertook any actions."

This is where I pause. I'm not telling him about his meeting with the mysterious Robert Finch nor Tad's increasing disillusion and despondency.

"And the PBF?" he adds, just a little too quietly, though it could be the stiff breeze blowing off the marina.

"I mentioned that you seemed most perturbed by those three letters. They didn't mean anything to me, but one of the others had come across the idea of tracking, through the year, amounts of bonus to be paid as a result of actions taken, corporate results and so on, and we deduced that PBF quite possibly meant Paid Bonus Factor."

So far so true. But, I did wonder whether Guillame had the internal connections to work out which one of the other two might have come across the idea during their working life. I felt increasingly unsettled.

"And that is basically it, in a nutshell."

Guillame pauses, momentarily.

"But why would this be unpleasant to you, Teddi?"

Ah, so this is it, I thought. The nub of the issue as far as he is concerned. We've wandered from the Promenade du Lac onto the Quai Gustave Ador, and as we gaze out over the yachts in the marina, and listen to sheets slapping against masts, I know I don't have to answer this. We are now comfortably off track. Having said that, what I may say is as unattributable as anything he has said so far.

Unless he is wearing a wire, that is. I banish that from my thoughts straight away: Tad's paranoia must be starting to rub off on me.

"Executive bonuses, executive pay. Well, where to start?"

I let out a deep sigh. On the marina boardwalk, at the cheap-end, a lone catamaran sailor is tidying away sheets and sails, no doubt after a satisfying mornings' sail on the lake. He is far too far away to hear a word we say – the nearest yacht wouldn't hear us, our voices are now so *sotto voce*.

For the first time I realize how conspiratorial we

must look. Guillame's double air kiss greeting suddenly feels less like a friendly hello and more like a Judas-like betrayal. I suddenly worry that an invitation to join the LTIP might be his thirty pieces of silver.

I can't submit to this paranoia, and I take a deep calming breath to steady my nerves.

"Look, the initial response has to focus on the changes to the Board paper. The paper carries my sign off, Arlene's, Tad's, heck yours, and others, so when the Board sees it they think that *we* have put it forward. But, we didn't, so it feels like our good names have been exploited in some way. There haven't been any facts available to explain why the changes were made – there could have been some highly credible commercial explanation, and though we would have preferred to know up front about this, we could probably get comfortable with the outcome. Provided that the numbers still stacked up, which isn't a given for tax, at least.

"However, the mention of PBF seemed to imply targets, and the combination seemed to imply that the decision-making process had been deliberately skewed, and this so that the Board could get a bigger bonus, and for no other reason."

"Now that truly unsettled us," I add.

I pause again. Guillame indicates with a nod of his head that we should wander a little more. I'm not surprised. This doesn't feel like a conversation we will end comfortably any time soon, certainly not before we get back to the office.

Chapter 34

"What do you think of executive pay in general, Teddi?" he asks. It's a question asked very casually, but weighted heavily. "Your little moue over lunch?" he adds as a reminder.

He smiles and I smile back, as much to break the tension as anything else. He's brought our conversation back to the market rate.

"Well it's a bit like your description of the reactions of the senior management team to the LTIP, when it was first proposed. Executive pay is out of hand, and I'm not just talking about bonuses."

He looks at me. I plough on.

"I once picked up a copy of a book about economic bubbles. It was first published in the 1800's, but is available in various reprints."

He is now looking a little bemused.

"It's a great book. I picked it up for its discussion about the South Sea Islands Bubble in the context of my MBA dissertation, but it goes way beyond that. It's really all about crowd psychology and financial markets, and places an analysis of capitalism firmly within that context."

His smile has gone. He pushes his sunglasses up into his hair, maybe to look jaunty, or at least less forbidding, but his smile has gone, replaced by deep concentration. His facial expression reminds me less of an urbane Milanese and more of a forbidding Jesuit.

I continue. Got no choice now.

"Ok let's look at this from another perspective. The way I see it, capitalism is a great force for change, a huge one, one of the biggest that we know. It creates opportunities and advancements, educates, heals, you get the picture. But, and this is a huge but, it isn't a moral force. I don't mean that it is immoral, in fact it is inherently neither evil nor good. It is simply a buy-sell arrangement, with no moral dimension to it at all. If there is a willing buyer for something, someone, somewhere will provide it. It is so simple, and also so complex. "

He is looking a little surprised now.

"The problems arise when we leave it alone. As a simple buy-sell, all sorts of things we don't like will get traded. What I like about the book I mentioned is that it shows, over and over again, how this happens. To my mind, the bubble in the price of technology stocks, or in property prices, has similarities with the bubble in the value of tulips bulbs nearly four hundred years earlier. Pyramid schemes keep on coming. Companies and individuals disappear with investors' money.

What strikes me is that we, as evolved humans, have learned, in some spheres, to guard against this. We stop children being exploited in factories and being sent up chimneys. We pass laws to protect children from paedophiles. But, we fail to stop human trafficking, forced prostitution, and forced slavery, so it is an ongoing battle. The battle is to recognize when the buy-sell is creating an outcome that isn't socially desirable, that we as evolved beings are not happy to accept. After that, the battle is to create consensus around what to do about it, and enforce it.

I look at this, Guillame, and wonder to what extent executive pay is just another of these situations?"

To Guillame's credit, he looks to be taking this very calmly.

"But executive pay is determined by the market, Teddi."

"And the senior management team themselves recognized that the market seems to be producing excess," I retort back.

"Quite so," he smiles back at me. "But that was only about the terms of that bonus scheme. You seem to be implying that this is generic across the piece."

"I guess I am. Executive pay has risen dramatically over the last ten years or so. A CEO might have gotten paid six hundred grand in the year 2000, but by 2010 this might have been four million. Or more. With bonuses and stock options and the like on top of that."

"Surely it can't have been that bad?"

"There is some research of actual pay packets that supports that very point. I'll dig out a link to the data that I found – it's available on the web – if it would help?"

He pauses. We have wandered a long way from the office, and somehow beyond the lake side walks.

We walk into a coffee shop together, as if by mutual, unspoken agreement, and order two ristrettos and water, and lean on a table, people watching. Clearly, he is thinking this over, but I'm glad of the break too; my new shoes are killing me, and I am dreading the walk back to the office. We make idle small talk about the weather, the opera advertised on a poster across the street, and the price of houses in Geneva these days. Most of

Guillame's team, at least those that have bought recently, have bought across the border in France and commute into Switzerland each day. Property purchases in Switzerland these days seem only for billionaires with specially-approved, reduced tax rate regimes. Guillame can't imagine bringing his family from Italy into that situation, and the cost of expat status for all of them sounds to be more than he feels asking the business to bear.

Not for the first time, I think of Em's sudden, impending departure, and realize just how vulnerable my role is also.

Chapter 35

Guillame must have noticed my shoe discomfort, for we head out of the café and turn into the Parc de la Grange. We settle on a bench, underneath a plane tree, set back from the main path, and with a clear view all around for anyone approaching.

"I gain the impression, Teddi, that despite your immense work load in the office you have managed to give considerable application of that great intellect of yours onto this subject."

I don't know if he is taking the mickey, or being straight. I play it straight.

"It's hard *not* to think about the big issues of our day. The way I see it, the current process revolves around reference to a market price for executives. Trouble is, everyone references the same headhunters and experts, and everyone wants to be seen to be doing a good job, so they all aim to be in the upper quadrant. They get their pay rise, they let the headhunters know, the headhunters factor the pay into their market data, and the effect of which is that the overall structure spirals upwards.

It gets worse. The non-executives, who should be protecting the shareholders, defer to the market (because, doesn't everyone?), as does the Remuneration Committee. So no-one acts for the shareholders, who see their returns being hammered by this spiral, with growth being battered by rising executive cost. In this situation, the shareholder isn't some gullible fool enticed by the prospect of easy money, as with Tulipomania, but is actively unable to gain control over proceedings."

"Are you saying that individual executives shouldn't be in those positions?" he asks sharply.

"Not at all, Guillame, the execs are just doing what the market is, in effect, telling them to do. But look at it like this."

I pause. I'm treading over the ground of my conversation with Arlene and Tad, but it isn't a re-run. It feels like that earlier conversation was a practice for this. This feels like a pivotal moment, like my life will evolve from here, depending on how this goes. I feel energized.

"Executives are not some precious, miracle breed that must be paid else all will be lost. Let's put it another way, if this were true then in twenty years or so the business world would be bereft of leadership when they all retire, which you and I both know is nonsense. There will always be someone waiting in the wings to take the top job, and that person will be willing to do it for less money, if that is what is required to get the role. It is the old buy-sell again, pure and simple. I reckon you could rein executive pay back to levels last seen in the year 2000. If anyone quibbles, well they know where the door is, but my guess is that most people would want to stay in situ. The business would get enormous kudos from investors."

Guillame is looking at me. His arm is across the back of the bench, one ankle crossed onto the other knee, sunglasses still perched in his immaculately coiffed hair. Maybe this is part of how he is so successful – pretty much utter control of body language no matter what the situation, no matter what the stakes.

"What about the investors? Would they be happy?"

"It's a good question, Guillame. It's the heart of the issue, really. Businesses do what they think investors want from them. They cut costs, or move factories say to the Ukraine. They open new markets in new locations. They buy and sell bits of themselves. They seek to be regarded as well run by their investors.

Investors, though, are both really sensible and really fickle. For example, they may want a well-run company, they may want executive pay under control, but there are investors aplenty who simply don't look to the five year horizon, but care only about dividends this year. The executive cadre becomes used to the idea. Investment decisions are made based on net present value analysis, but at the end of the day investors can be fickle about decisions made. If three quarters of the players in a business have closed their USA factory and opened one in the Far East, then investors will clamour for the last few to follow suit. This even though it is apparent that it is a nil-sum game, at the end of the day. Eventually all costs rise, and the last few may actually have the delivery and innovation advantage of having retained factories located close to established markets.

Like I say, these short term and sometimes shallow views must certainly be recognized as contributing to if not actually causing the situation to arise. Heck, there are banks and hedge funds out there that own more oil on the high seas than the producers or sellers, just holding onto it to force prices up, make profits, pay their bonuses, and screw everyone else. Like over-arching and uncontrolled oligopolies, pummeling governments through their borrowing costs whilst fixing the markets in their favour, with individual governments and regulators either incapable of or unwilling to challenge."

"So you think we should regulate the capital markets, Teddi? Isn't that anti-capitalist, anti-business?" He tries to sound casual, but there is a sharpness to his tone that I haven't heard before. Not very strong, but there, subtly underlining his overt casualness. There is a hint to be taken.

"We always do, Guillame, you should know that. When humanity perceives the markets have gone awry. It's why countries have competition policies. I'm not talking about control by some form of communist fiat – politicians frequently give the impression of being as incapable of resisting the dangers of power as hedge fund and bank CEOs, so that is just plain crazy. But we have to be capable of preventing the abuses of position that are currently taking place. Economic theory is being proven to be correct right in front of our faces – a small few can dominate markets, and whether working formally together to rig interest rates, or informally to drive asset prices, markets are being abused. Pure and simple. The market is not open and informed, it is not full of equal buyers and sellers, when markets can be manipulated in this way. Market dominance of this form is what is anti-capitalist and anti-business."

"But how does a government control a hedge fund, or a bank, when the bank contributes to GDP and the government is up to its eye balls in debt? When the bank 'owns' the government in some way? When the banker is another country? How does a government control its banker?"

"Ah Guillame, now we are onto the current global debt crisis: Remedies for Global Crisis 101."

Guillame does a double-take, but then he bursts into a smile whilst genuinely looking relaxed. Drifting across the back of my mind, barely acknowledged, I wonder if we are finally getting to the meat of this afternoon's conversation.

"Recession and debt crises? Really? This I want to hear, Teddi, this I want to hear."

He is laughing, but his eyes are appraising me, warning me yet again that this conversation is no idle chat opportunity. We aren't shooting the breeze to kill time, even though the afternoon is hurtling by.

There is a whole lot more going on here than he has so far acknowledged.

Chapter 36

The sound of a school bell, and the ensuing chatter of young voices, slice into our conversation, as if to remind us of the precious nature of our time together. It's time to pick up the threads again.

"In a way, the current global debt crisis is telling us that we, as a species, have reached a turning point."

I pause to let this sink in. I recall a politician who took pains to speak clearly, whether introducing himself to strangers in a clear, slow voice, or explaining his point in a discussion. In some ways it was a courtesy, both to his listener, to ensure that they understood, but also to himself, to do his words justice. I realize that Guillame does it. I decide to do it too, speaking slowly, pausing here and there, and speaking relatively quietly.

"We have allowed a largely unregulated capitalist model to reach its epitome. Governments are mired in debt, with a wing and a prayer hope that GDP will suddenly grow to pay it all off, and in the meantime cowed by those who own their debt, whether banks, hedge funds, venture capitalists or cash rich countries.

Businesses are mired in debt, desperate to both grow income and reduce cost, in some cases with the whole executive pay trauma thrown in for good measure, but hoarding their cash, unwilling to spend it 'just in case', like French investors in the aftermath of the Mississippi Scheme four hundred years ago.

Households have cut costs to the bone, resorting to payday loans and worse to make their monthly income stretch.

Politicians stick their heads in the sand, redefining inflation so that it doesn't show the true pain to households, whilst drawing their salaries, submitting their expense claims, and setting up yet more quangos to 'consider issues,' and spending a small fortune to run them. A few more jobs for career civil servants appear, whilst easy targets are cut from civil service budgets. Maybe the politicians bleat their empathy and wring their hands, but what long-term, structural solutions are proposed?"

Guillame is looking at the ground now. Face still, betraying no particular emotions or thoughts. Concentrating.

I let a smartly uniformed nanny and three neatly attired schoolchildren walk by before continuing.

"But the global financial markets are beyond huge, Teddi. How can any government or business put forward a solution that will control seven-hundred-trillion dollars of financial assets? "

"I think you've just hit the nail on the head, Guillame. That's the whole point. Individual politicians, political parties, Boards of business, don't stand a chance against the massive casino that is the financial markets."

"So what is your point? Aren't you just contradicting yourself?"

"No, not when you consider the difference between solutions put forward so far, and those that could be advocated," I suggest.

He considers this.

"You think that what has been put forward so far doesn't work, or won't in the future even if it does today?"

"Something like that, Guillame. Quantitative easing pumps billions, trillions, into the financial markets themselves, but at the cost of destroying long term assets like returns on bonds. That means that pensioners current and future see their pension values collapse. Not just that, think of all of the plumbers, electricians, engineers, nurses that could have been trained for that money, think of the industrial infrastructure that could have been put in place for that money, think of the true wealth of a nation that could have been created in countries across the globe. It's a shoddy business, and it hasn't worked. It is failing even now, and will continue to fail."

I've spoken harshly, and he is looking a little taken aback.

"Take bond rescues of banks and nations like Greece and Spain, and future rescues, all to prop up the Euro. It is physically impossible for one European country, or a central European bank or body, to bankroll financial bets that take on and beat global markets."

"But this we know, Teddi. This is why there is a push to see financial unity across the Euro, if not political unity also."

"And will that really sustain, Guillame? How many times have the nation states of Europe risen up against one state that tries to control them? And for what? To sustain the Euro, and perhaps the export markets of Germany?

Why don't we think about it from the German perspective? If you talk to the average German on the street, how many will agree with what is being proposed by their political leaders? Thirty percent? Twenty percent? And how many just want to trade with the rest of the world and enjoy a peaceful life? How many wish that there wasn't this minority with a fetish for controlling people?

Think about it from the perspective of a rescued nation like Greece. How many nation states in say Africa have struggled for years with debt levels that are so high, their country never can rebuild and the debts will never be repaid? Do we wish this for Greece, for Spain, for whoever is next in the firing line of the financial markets?"

"But they cannot default, Teddi, that would destroy their standing."

I look him in the eye, just for a moment or two, so that he knows that he is being listened to.

"Look at it another way, Guillame. What would happen if central banks defaulted on their 'quantitative easing bonds?' I guess their argument runs that no-one would be really hurt by it, so why not.

But think about the consequences, Guillame. Those nations that have been struggling under a mountain of debt for decades would look at this and say, well if they can do it, we can do it too.

The nations newly drowning in debt would do the same, as would businesses and individuals. It would be carnage.

How could a central bank say "this is ok for me to do, but you mustn't?' with a straight face and not expect disastrous consequences?"

"But, Teddi, that it why default must be out of the question." Guillame is sounding frustrated now. "Where are you going with this line of reasoning?"

"Because default is only out of the question at a unilateral level," I reply, and watch as this sinks in.

“Multilateral default, planned meticulously amidst great secrecy, enacted by statesmen working in concert, would work. At the same time, connect it with a pre-planned wind down of the Euro, and implementation of several key restraints on financial markets. Leadership with a new way of behaving. A new world order.”

Chapter 37

Guillame jaw has dropped, but he recovers very fast.

"Multilateral debt write offs? How?"

"It would have to involve all the major nations, though probably not cash-rich banker nations. It would have to use some recent, historic point, such as the previous 31st December, but it would have to be one where businesses and governments could not rig their financial accounts to avoid manipulation of positions.

It would have to be a significant proportion in order to make a difference, but not enough to trigger a global, inflationary wildfire. Maybe half? And it would have to protect the innocent, like those pensioners relying on savings to survive."

"Just like that?"

"Yup. Anything is possible if people put their minds to it, Guillame. Think about how much time and intellectual capital has been expended over the last few years on protecting the Euro. Imagine if it had been spent on this project instead. All too often, people can inhabit an environment for so long that they become complacent, forget how it looks from the outside. I truly believe that this is possible, that this would have a truly liberating effect on the global economy."

I add, "Of course, it would take statesmen,

leaders of men."

"There is a difference between the leaders we have now, and those we would need?"

"Not necessarily, but probably. It's the same conversation about Board behavior writ large, Guillame. There may well be leaders in businesses, in Governments, who can switch rapidly and drop all sense of their former self, and embrace the new way of being with gusto. Equally, and I suspect more probably, there will be individuals waiting in the wings for just an opportunity like this. Individuals with a sense of vision untainted by the scandals that have gotten us to this point. Individuals who aren't all about their ego and their paycheck, but are true leaders of men, able to step beyond the petty boundaries that people and governments have drawn around themselves.

Think about it Guillame. Why did the printers of the Gutenberg Bible decided to create those books? I'll tell you. To free mankind. To give mankind the opportunity to think for itself and reach for its highest ideals. Did they really do that so that, one day, a person's life would be measured solely by the size of their salary or their bonus? Is this the sum total of our evolutionary journey as human beings?"

I pause for breath.

"Let us be very clear about this, Guillame, Entire nation states are imploding under the weight of this crisis. There are millions and millions of people for whom this is not acceptable, and who look to their leaders for a way forward, and get nothing back." I'm thinking of Katie and her fruitless struggle to find a job and pay her way, and of the millions globally in her position.

"This is a once-in-a-lifetime chance to make positive change, maybe even a pivotal moment in the evolution of humans, but is that opportunity being grasped? Or is it being dodged so that things carry on, as they are, for one more day? For how long will King Canute be in charge, for how long must we lumber forward blind, without vision?"

Guillame is looking at me, but, surprisingly, he doesn't look frustrated or uptight anymore.

"Where have these ideas come from, Teddi?"

"My head," I laugh ruefully. "Back in spring 2009 I was all for cutting costs and taxes. By spring 2010 I knew that wasn't enough and was all for a tidy exit from the Euro. By spring 2011, I was for multilateral debt write-offs, and now? By now I have realized that to implement it all we need a radical change in how our leaders behave. And I can't be the only one thinking like this."

"You seem very specific about dates?"

"Well Guillame, this may be news to you, but I could haul friends in front of you who would roll their eyes and say 'Oh, she isn't blathering on about that again, is she? Can't you make her stop?'"

And I laugh ruefully again, and to his credit so does Guillame.

"So I've been warned?"

"Ah don't worry, I won't say it all again. Take too long anyway."

We both glance at our watches. Time has really flown by. It's getting on for five pm and we are a long way from the office. As if by unspoken mutual agreement we get up and start to walk back to the road. My feet are killing me – blisters must have been developing quite nicely as we sat on the bench. With each step, pain shoots up from my little toes and my heels and I am struggling not to hobble. Guillame notices. That didn't work.

"Let's get a taxi back?"

“Fabulous idea,” I reply gratefully, and he calls on his mobile for a taxi.

Chapter 38

We're idling on the kerb, waiting for our taxi to appear. I'm suddenly feeling shattered, from a mix of good food, warm sunshine, and a heavy dose of the kind of stimulating conversation that destroys brain cells by the million.

"Just one final thought, Teddi. You mentioned controls on financial markets. Is it really possible to implement these? The history of wage control policies would suggest not."

Oh dear. Right now I really need vacuous small talk, polite chit-chat and empty observation. The kind of fluff that my brain can pootle over whilst re-charging. Clearly, though, the conversation isn't over yet. I haul my mental faculties back together again before replying.

"I think so, Guillame, as long as they're carefully drawn. For example, ban short selling." He looks startled again, but before he can say anything I continue. "We have had temporary bans in place before, and they do work, but a temporary ban merely makes the markets bide their time until the ban is lifted, and lobby hard for that to happen as soon as possible. A permanent ban? Now that would be interesting. Stop a lot of crazy volatility in its tracks. As we said before, the markets are proving that they are not efficient, that oligopolies, and worse, exist, and that they have developed traits and behaviours that are not in mankind's interests."

He's waving to the cab as it approaches.

"Thing is, Guillame, I can only see one drawback: what would everyone do with this sudden increase in spending power, this sudden release of cash? Would governments spend on armaments, and would a new wave of hostilities break out? Would people splurge again on houses, holidays and all that jazz? Could this trigger a new wave of debt-funded consumerism? A whirling dervish of a storm that would spin faster and wilder than the one we have just lived through? Are we simply going to end up back where we are now?"

"Based upon the empirical evidence of the last twenty years, Teddi? I would say that this is the most likely outcome, although I would be delighted if we could learn our lessons."

He looks at me, with the wryest of smiles.

"Am I talking myself out of a great idea?" I smile back.

He laughs.

"Unless you're telling me you have another?"

"Well," I begin, "I did have *one* more."

We're climbing into the cab now.

"What if there was a way to move beyond all of this ugliness, once and for all?"

I'm musing, really, voicing a thought that has begun to lurk in the back of my mind.

He nods, as if to encourage. We're relaxing into the seats as the car starts to move smoothly forward, and I'm arranging my tender feet in the way that applies least pressure to what I'm guessing are by now substantial blisters.

"What if debt didn't exist? What if all you could ever buy would be out of your assets, savings and earnings? What if growth was steady and sustainable?"

Guillame is holding my gaze now.

"It's the obvious things that bug me. Take usurious payday loans. What if they were a thing of the past? I mean, why do they even exist? Why haven't they been abolished off the face of the planet? And how are we, the young workers of the planet, ever supposed to pay off the debts the baby boomers have run up to fund their pensions and the past twenty years of excess? In fact, how is an employee on average pay ever supposed to fund a meaningful pension, come to that? Do you know, there is some statistic around that the average worker will earn one and a half million dollars over their life, but would have to put aside forty per cent of that to pay for a pension? So they get to live on around nine hundred thousand. Sounds a lot, till you realize that has to sustain them over fifty years, and they've got to pay taxes too. The average worker would have eighteen thousand dollars each year to pay taxes, pay a mortgage or rent, buy food, pay utilities, all of that good stuff. In other words, live on the breadline, if not lower than that. And if that is all that people have to spend, the entire economy will, eventually contract, as governments are unable to raise enough taxes to pay for the schools, hospitals and so on that those workers need. It's a positively Dickensian prospect."

"At the political level, there is a real fear that the developed world could descend into chaos, Teddi."

Guillame doesn't sound surprised by this analysis, he doesn't even seem to disagree.

"Based upon all this no doubt," I reply. "But surely teetering along the existing tightrope just defers chaos into the future, by a few years? This can't be the final point in our evolutionary journey, Guillame, so where are the new paradigms to help us move forward? Abolishing debt could be the vision that we need to work towards."

"I think the definitions would be hard work."

"Only if you allow endless lawyering, Guillame. Nickel-and-dimeing whilst the global economy implodes is what humans are very good at. It would have to be an absolute that the vision couldn't be lawyered away. "

"Ah, that vision thing again, Teddi," he replies. "What is it like to be able to see the sunny uplands?"

He is smiling, but his smile is gentle and genuine. Encouraging. Luckily enough at that, else I might have thought he was taking the mickey.

"Ah, you know, sometimes I love it, and sometimes I think it is just a right royal pain in the ass. I mean, what is the point of it? Who is interested? Can't earn a living with it; it doesn't fit in any neat corporate pigeon-holes."

I smile ruefully back at him.

"Just one more thought, Guillame."

"Yes?" He looks more relaxed now.

"Earlier, you said that these are dangerous times. Dangerous for whom, Guillame? For me? Do I need to be afraid?"

He seems to waver slightly in his seat. I sit, waiting for his reply.

"For everyone, Teddi, at least until the changes I refer to take place."

"But if they are to take place, then the danger can only be transient in nature, and reversible," I counter. "Unless the changes are not guaranteed to happen."

Of course. That's it. Part of the reason that he isn't telling me about these changes is that they aren't set in stone yet. I shiver despite the warm June afternoon sunshine – someone walking across my grave, my gran used to call it. Maybe he is trustworthy, maybe he isn't, but he isn't certain of delivering the outcome.

He shrugs lightly. No, there is nothing I can do about it, it's just the way things are right now, he seems to say. In the lap of the gods.

We're somehow dodging the traffic and hurtling back toward the office. Amazing how quickly you can drive a route that took so long to walk.

"Guillame. Back there, when I was talking about excess?" I glance nervously toward the driver, and Guillame picks up that this is probably going to be in discreet code rather than stated upfront. "I wasn't including you in that group. More the waiting in the wings group. I hope you understood that? That I made that clear?"

"Don't worry, Teddi, I had understood that." He reaches into his pocket and passes me his card. "Look, if you need to speak to me, give me a call. I'm best reached on this number" (he scribbles a number next to all of the other contact information).

"My PA doesn't have access to that one," he adds, as we pull up outside the office. "Elisabeth is amazing, but she's a formidable barrier. Great when I need that, but sometimes I find that I need more *fluid* access. Use that cell number."

"Thanks, Guillame."

Chapter 40

Back in my office, I kick off my shoes and sink gratefully into my chair. No, I shouldn't have taken them off, all the walking guides in the world say to keep your boots on if you have a blister, at least until you can treat it. But I am knackered. Footsore and brain aching. Plus my gym trainers are in a bag in a cupboard.

The afternoon's conversation is whirling around in my head. I don't know what is planned, but I do now know that the changes to the paper were deliberate, implemented by a minority, and designed purely to boost bonus payout. I'm supposed to be briefing Tad and Arlene in a call tomorrow afternoon, but I decide not to wait, give them each a quick debrief call so they can think about things ahead of the main discussion tomorrow.

Tad's cell bounces to voicemail, and I leave a casual 'just getting in touch' message. I call his landline; this bounces to his PA, Jagde.

"Hey Jagde, it's Teddi. Is Tad around? I've tried his cell but can't raise him."

There is a quiet for a moment, then her words tumble out.

"I'm sorry, Teddi, Tad isn't here. He's got some business to attend to. I don't know where exactly, and I don't know when he will be back. Sorry, I can't help."

O-kay. I play it lightly.

"Can I leave a message, ask him to call me when he returns from wherever he is right now?"

"I'd rather not, Teddi. Is there anything else I can help you with?"

Beg pardon? His PA isn't taking a message for him? Weird.

"No, nothing else, Jagde. Have a great day."

And she hangs up, without even saying goodbye.

I place a call to Arlene. Please let her be there, I'm thinking, I really don't need weirdness with these guys after my afternoon's grilling by Guillame.

"Hey Arlene, it's Teddi. Do you have five minutes for a quick debrief about Guillame?"

"Teddi, I am glad to hear from you. I've had three different guys on the phone today who've been trying to get hold of Tad, and can't raise him. I've tried, I can't raise him. This is really unlike him."

"I've tried too, Arlene," I interject. "And his PA gave me the brush off when I asked about him. Point-blank rude she was. What's going on?"

"No idea, but…" Arlene replies, and we both fill in the rest of it. This paper business has somehow caught up with Tad. Suddenly it feels like someone has left open a door, somewhere in my life, and a stiff breeze is blowing in.

"Arlene, I have no idea where this is all headed, but the news from Guillame isn't good, and you need to know it. His research shows that the Board paper was changed by a minority purely to boost bonus payouts. Things are afoot that he won't tell me about, but they aren't certain to happen."

"Are we safe, Teddi?"

"Who the hell knows, Arlene? That's the million dollar question. Oh look, I'm sorry, I didn't mean to be rude and swear. Truth is, I asked Guillame that very question, and he couldn't say we were. Safe that is. Said everyone was at risk, unless and until the big changes he referred to took place."

"So, basically, you and I could be looking at anything, all the way to job loss, potentially?"

"That's the way I read it."

"Damn and darnation."

"Bloody awful, is how I would describe it. Look, Arlene, I can't tell you what to do. For me, I'm going to contemplate today's events, and be ready to talk with you and Tad tomorrow afternoon. And I think I need to go for a long run tonight."

"Either that or a stiff drink. Maybe this calls for a long one, Teddi?"

"Ah, maybe you're right."

"Speak tomorrow, Teddi."

"Yeah, speak tomorrow, Arlene."

I've had enough of today. I need to get out of the office and think about all of this, flip it over with Christoph, maybe get some perspectives and insights about how to play this next. I'm putting on my gym shoes when Brett appears in my office doorway.

"Ah Teddi, delightful, glad you are still here. Could you just join us in the conference room? Won't take a moment, but could do with your presence on something, what?"

Shit. Talk about the devil. My nemesis in all his glory. I look down at my shoes.

"Err…"

"No matter, Teddi, no matter. Let's get going, soonest started, soonest sorted."

With which he zooms back along the corridor at

a startling pace. I grab my meeting folio (always stocked with a notepad and pen) and shoot after him, trainers and all, into the conference room.

Where, I'm taken aback. It's virtually a full house for the Kingdom deal team. Brett, Johann, Guillame, the lawyers, various second-in-commands. The sqwawkbox for teleconferencing is placed near Brett.

"Ah Teddi, do sit down. Glad you can be here. Don't worry about this" (he gestures to the sqwawkbox) "it isn't on."

At this point I feel distinctly uneasy, because it very much *is* on – I can see the 'on' light reflected in the face of his watch. Who the hell is on the other end of the line?

I turn to face Guillame. He is staring at his note pad, suddenly deeply absorbed by what he can see there. No eye contact.

"Anyway, glad you can be here. As you know, the economic climate is very tough, and we have been discussing ways that we on the Kingdom deal can reduce costs for our part."

That must have been quick, I reflect inwardly. Guillame can only have been in the room for ten minutes. Either this was all pre-agreed, or it was an ambush.

"What do you have in mind Brett? A reduction in flights? Switching to cheaper seats?" It's a cheap shot, and I'm embarrassed to have taken it, but something inside me is glad to have said it anyway. Publicly pointed out his largesse.

"Something deeper than that, Teddi. We've reflected on the resources that we need to finish the deal. Tad, we have realized, is an expert of deep value to the business, and we are wasting his time, now that he has finished his report. He is being seconded to Malaysia, to be Country MD."

Ambush. Got to be. That can't have been set up in ten minutes. And you have to admire Brett's guile – move Tad, and there is no-one present to push back against Brett's attempts to move the decision-making goalposts on operational matters. It's a masterstroke. Shitty, but a masterstroke.

"When will that take effect, Brett?"

"Well, he is discussing the practical steps with HR right now. I believe he will be on seat by Monday, and his family will follow in the summer recess."

Dear god. That is *fast*.

"And how can I help, Brett? Do you need input on his expat package?"

Someone in the room titters, nervously, then gulps it down.

"Not quite, Teddi. We also realize that you are similarly valuable to the business. The work you have done is absolutely top class, and we have a great implementation plan…"

"Which won't work if anything changes in the operational plan."

"Ah Teddi, you underestimate yourself. I have every confidence that with all of the fine work that you have done for us in getting us ready for the future, implementation plans will be capable of adjustment as needed. Every confidence."

I'm speechless. I shoot Guillame a look. He is still staring at his notepad, though I think I can detect an uncharacteristic, faint hint of pink to his olive cheeks.

I turn back to Brett. Not just my nemesis, but my executioner.

"And what do you have in mind exactly, Brett?"

"Well, you can hand over to the two who work for Hans in the Swiss domestic team. That can't take long, I'm sure that Hans will support them as needed. HR will want to discuss your redeployment within the business. Of course it isn't for us to decide how you would most optimally be employed, though I note that we are starting to send expats away from head office and back to their home countries. We do of course wish you all the very best and thank you for your wonderful guidance, with which we can now progress."

He smiles his snake smile – lips moving, but eyes static and dangerous. The fucking shit. I feel like I've been punched in my gut. I look around the table. Everyone avoids my eyes. To their credit most look ashamed, though maybe that is just my, by now, very prejudiced interpretation.

I pull myself up in my seat, and "do a Millie." Years ago, a friend told me how her great-grandmother had moved to India after marriage. Though the Raj had ended, social circles were still very much full of deeply condescending and imperious women attempting to behave in the Edwardian mould who took every chance to put others down. She had hated it. Whilst her husband was at work she had to mix with these women and would dread going into their company.

So she had developed a strategy. As she entered a room she would imagine putting on a stout pair of shoes and tying the laces very soundly, pulling them tight so she could walk confidently into the room. We decided that whenever we felt ourselves in need of courage we would imagine being Mille, pulling up our shoe laces and striding confidently forward.

So I "did a Millie."

"Ladies, gentlemen. It has been a pleasure working with you. I hope and trust that this project will move forward with the success that it deserves, and I wish you all the very best for your future careers. It's been a pleasure to get to know you. Now, is there anything else I can help you with, Brett?"

I turn to him and smile. I actually feel like shit, but I'm determined that he, and they, won't see this.

"No, that's it Teddi."

"Well if that's all, I'll get back to my office."

And with that, I nod to the room, stand up and walk out the door. I walk to my office, grab my bag, turn around, and walk straight out.

Fucking hell.

Chapter 41

Afterwards, I don't recall my drive home. Somehow, I'm opening the door of my apartment, and as I do the enormity of the last few hours finally hits home. The numbness wears off, and I stand in the hallway bewildered and shaking, great tears rolling unchecked down my cheeks and off my jaw.

The ringing phone startles me, and I wonder for a moment why my blouse collar feels so soggy. I look in the mirror; it's sodden with tears and streaked with mascara.

The caller is Christoph. He must be wondering what has happened – I promised to call once my lunch was over. Lunch. Good grief. That seems an age ago now.

"Hello darling, it's me."

"Hello Christoph," I reply. Or at least I think I do, but whether he understands a word between sobs is probably debatable.

"So, that bad?"

"Worse, worse than you can imagine," and I burst into tears again. "Sorry, sorry, I didn't mean to do that," I mumble, wiping tears and snot onto the back of my hand as I stumble into the bathroom and fumble for loo roll.

"I'll be there in half an hour. Wait for me." And he hangs up.

True to his word, the doorbell rings half an hour later. My suit lies abandoned on my bed, though trainers and bag are still in the hall way. I've attempted to tidy myself up (put on a dress, splashed my face with cold water then perfume) and stacked hankies and loo roll all over the place. But it's a waste of time really – my eyes are bloodshot, the skin around them dry and crepey like an eczema sufferers' and the end of my nose is red raw after thirty minutes-plus of hard core nose-blowing.

I feel like shit, look worse and open the door to Christoph vaguely aware that I'm not sure how he will take this. The hope is that love will greet me, but I'm not sure. So much has turned upside down over the last few weeks, I feel like I'm walking on quick sand half the time. This is probably the first crisis that we have faced as a couple.

I needn't have worried. He quietly steps forward and puts his arms around me, pulling me tightly into him and holding me there. Holding me as new tears flow, and until they fade and I quieten and calm. Only then does he loosen his grip, close the door behind us with one arm, and guide me through to the sofa.

Feeling pathetic and weak, but also hugely grateful and somehow safe, on a small grassy hillock in a vast moorland bog, I sit and watch him unload a bag he has been carrying (how? how many arms does he have?). It's a take-out Chinese and a bottle of wine – comfort food nirvana. How have I anglicised him?

I'm borderline blubbing again, and he glances at me.

"No, not another deluge, just happiness, human joy. Thank you, Christoph. Love you, handsome."

I wipe my face, and we both smile.

"Would you look at me? What a mess."

"I love you however you are," he smiles, and passes me a glass of Riesling and my sweet 'n' sour chicken with egg fried rice.

"Cheers."

"Zum wohl."

It's amazing how your spirits lift when you no longer feel alone.

Not much later, we're cuddling on the sofa, and Christoph finally points to the elephant in the room.

"So, gorgeous, what happened today?"

I tell him everything, right up to clearing out of the office. He doesn't say a word during my monologue. No interruptions, no suggestions, no comments or homilies. Just listens, occasionally nodding or squeezing my hand.

"Hell of a day," he ventures when I finish.

"And how."

"What is your take?"

"Dunno. I'm still in shock, really."

"There are lots of ways to interpret what has happened, Teddi," he begins. "Maybe Guillame knew about your exit, maybe he didn't. He knew about Tad – that's why he tried to warn you, and yes, one purpose of the lunch was to warn you. "

He pauses to savour the wine.

"The revelations about the changes to the paper suggest he is on the level – he wouldn't tell you otherwise – but he isn't in control, at least not yet. He hopes to be."

"He does?"

"Mmmn, yes, he tried to tell you that too."

"Ok, well that is interesting, but why *me*, of all people?"

"You're an ally? Part of the future? Or at least not a threat."

"Doesn't feel like it right now, trust me. Not just off the deal, but being redeployed and possibly sent back to the UK."

"That is the point of weakness, I would say."

"Really?" This is good stuff. Christoph is seeing this from a detached position, one step removed. I heard the noise, saw everyone ignoring me, didn't twig that Brett could be on weak ground.

"How so? What do you see, Christoph?"

He takes another sip.

"First point. It is inconceivable for a project lead to tell someone they are losing their job. Off the project, sure, but changing job? No. That has to come from the line manager. What's his name? Hans? Maybe HR at a push.

He pauses to sip his wine, then continues.

"Second point. To do this in open court, in front of others, is also a no-no. It should have been done privately, which tells us that he was making a point, I think to everyone else in the room. At an educated guess, I'd say he was letting them know what would happen if they crossed him. And yes, Teddi, you've crossed him; perhaps he has found out some of what you guys have been up to? Maybe he's one of those "if you're not with me, you're against me" types? However and whatever, he's decided to make an example of you, irrespective of the niceties.

Third point, it worked, and it worked because of the open mike in the room. At a guess, again, I'd say that the other guy was on the line. What's his name? Arnold?"

"Armand," I reply quietly.

"So the weak point is the employment law aspect. He's broken virtually every rule in the book, and must be gambling on speed and surprise. Hans cannot know about this, or if he does, he doesn't know about the redeployment."

"Good points, but what do I do? You know what has happened to Em – this could move extremely swiftly. I could be back in the UK without a job in weeks. I mean, at least she has a role organised to go back to."

I'm feeling glum.

"This isn't set in stone yet, and what you do could make a difference to the outcome. Nothing rash and nothing that anyone could hold against you. But you do need to act. You need to play this innocent and straight, but you do need to play it. This is not the time to stick your head in the sand."

"Such as?"

"Well, the first thing to do is call Hans and leave a message, indicating that you've been told by Brett you're off the project and your role is changing, you may even be going home. Suggest that you've probably got the wrong end of the stick, you're a bit confused about what's going on, and ask if could you have five minutes with him tomorrow morning. It will get him thinking – if he is even half way as smart as you think, the employment law aspects will occur to him. He won't know exactly what has been going on, but he will be forewarned to think around whatever he gets told by this Brett guy."

"OK, I'll do that, but what about Guillame? What about Arlene? What about Tad?"

"Forget about Tad. He's history. He's been bought off with a promotion."

"What? But…"

"A great promotion and a pay rise. He probably doesn't even know it's connected to this issue. Just hasn't got in touch because he has been so busy with the move. When he does, you'll be long gone. That'll be the plan, anyway."

Blimey. I must look confused and more than a little taken aback.

"Just because we science boffins are on a government wage doesn't mean that we don't have to face our fair share of office politics. Seen it all before. Not the same bucks," he glances at me, "but all the same problems. Don't forget, the world is made up of people, and wherever you go, you meet the psychopaths, the egotists, the back-stabbers, the narcissists."

A fair point.

"Not too sure about your friend Arlene, though. You might want to leave her a message in the morning. Be coy, circumspect, but let her know that you know about what has happened to Tad. If she calls as soon as she gets the message, then I'd guess that she doesn't know. Equally, if she waits until this scheduled teleconference then she probably already does and is playing it innocent. Either way, she may well have career news for you."

"Are you sure about that analysis, Christoph? I really don't have that view of Arlene."

"Maybe you're right" he concedes. "But still, playing it this way will give you cover, just in case you're about to see that friendship disappear also."

"Hope not. I really like her. Really respect her, you know?"

But he's right. At the moment I have to play things cautiously.

"Which leaves two more important calls."

"It does?"

"Sure."

"Am all ears. Shoot."

"The first is your friend Em. You need to discover more about the circumstances surrounding her removal back to The Netherlands.

Has she been informed about some head office programme to reduce costs? Does she know of any other departees?"

"OK. Think I'll do that face to face, call round her office for a chat. Actually, I'm seeing her tomorrow evening for a catch up boozy session anyway. Maybe leave it till then? More subtle?"

"Not sure you can afford the delay."

Cripes. Good point though. I haven't heard of any departures from other central teams. Maybe I'm meant to be the one that makes both seem above board.

"Will see what I can do. And the final call, who is that to?"

"Guillame. The final piece in the jigsaw."

"Guillame? We're not sure yet what his position is. Isn't a call right now a bit dangerous?"

"Teddi, think about it. You're about to be booted out of head office. Hans will probably speak with Brett in very short order, and he will probably call around the project team to get some background on the change before formulating a response. Most people will, or ought, to be embarrassed, but they will refer it back to Brett. But not Guillame. He knows. And Hans won't buy it that everyone just simply deferred to Brett at such short notice over something so fundamental."

"But what do I say? Pitch this badly and I could shoot myself in the foot. If today has just been one joined up operation to find out what I know before dumping me, if he has been in on the move all along, then what I say won't matter, as long as I'm polite like you say. But if, and this is a big if, there is some bigger game going on behind the scenes, then I need him to know that I am still on board."

"Agreed. Leave him a message. Say you appreciate his position, that he was trying to warn you, and that you understand he was unable to do anything about it. Wish him well for the future."

"He won't interpret that as biased, one-sided?"

"But your discussions so far have been, anyway, right? It'll place you how you want, Teddi."

"Right. Look, Christoph, just one final thought. What do you think Guillame made of all of my off the cuff comments about bonuses and the global economy?"

"Maybe he took the comments about pay to heart, but you covered yourself on the way back to the office in the cab, right? If it was all a set up, then he'll probably write the time off and ignore what you said. If there is some behind the scenes activity, he may take more note. But you don't know what is going on, so why worry about that? Nothing you can do about it now."

"Would you have talked like that? In the same situation?"

"No, but I'm not you, Teddi. Your unstoppable creativity one of the very reasons that I find you so attractive."

"Hold that thought. I need to make some calls, but hold that thought. We need to explore it in greater depth…."

"Better make those calls then."

And with that I pick up my cell and leave two short messages, one to Hans' business mobile and one to Guillame's personal cell.

Then we finish the wine and turn our attentions to where it really matters. Each other.

Chapter 42

For the first time in a long time I'm not in the office for seven thirty. Not even close. Christoph has woken me up (I've slept the sleep of the dead since we talked), and afterwards made us breakfast (hot, strong, black coffee, smoked salmon, scrambled eggs and toast) so I don't roll in until gone half eight, a fraction before my contracted start time. Everyone else seems to be in.

I'm still hanging my jacket up when Hans appears at the doorway. He must have been watching for my arrival. He walks in and closes the door.

"Teddi, I got your voicemail."

"Hans, thank you, appreciate your time."

"What is going on?" he interrupts. "I walked into the office this morning to messages from you, Brett, Johann, Guillame, HR…"

"Wish I knew," I reply. "Brett calls me into a meeting yesterday at about quarter past five. Most of the Kingdom deal team seem to be there. The speakerphone is live, though Brett doesn't introduce whoever is on the other end of the line, and in fact states that there is no-one there. Brett announces two team changes, one of which is that I am off the team, and the work from here will be picked up by your compliance team, with your overview. Plus, and get this, I am to be redeployed.

So not just off the team, but out of a job. Then I was asked to leave the room again. I was back in my office within ten minutes, tops."

"But that doesn't make any sense at all, Teddi. The compliance people can't pick this up. They have absolutely no experience in this field, I don't have time for something like this, and our other advisers all have a full workload. That's why you're here, to develop that part of our team's offering, stop us relying so much on external advisers."

He pauses for thought, and then adds "Has something gone wrong on the project?"

"That's the whole point," I reply. "I'm performing extremely well on it. My work can't be faulted."

"Have you upset Brett?"

"No. But Hans, even if I had, his response would have to be described as utterly disproportionate."

"Fair comment. Then what?"

"We-ell...there is something. Nothing I've done wrong, I hasten to add, but something you should be considering."

"What does that mean?"

"Remember the recent Board paper for the project? Seeking final Board approval to implement?"

"Sure."

"You should have received two emails from Armand's PA with two versions of the paper."

"What of it?"

"Did you ever read through them, compare them side by side?"

"No, why should I? I just thought the first one probably contained typos. Didn't think anything of it."

"Then I suggest you take a very good look at them. Both of them. The second one is the version that the team signed off on prior to submission by Brett and Armand. The first? Well, it contains massive factual differences, like which factory to close, ideas alien to everything that that team had put forward. The temp PA for Armand tried to recall it."

"Are you suggesting that it was changed covertly? That's absurd, Teddi."

"Two things, Hans. Firstly, I discussed the changes with Arlene and Tad. Tad has been suddenly posted to Malaysia and I am off the team. Secondly, Guillame has done some background research, and confirms it."

"Guillame? Guillame Arnolfini? Head of Intellectual Property?"

"The one and the same. I suggest you speak to him before you speak with Brett, Johann, Human Resources or anyone else for that matter."

Hans is looking steadily at me now. His face can be impassive and inscrutable, like carved stone, but he has massive bandwidth, with an absolute supercomputer for a brain. He'll be processing chess moves, like working out how I know that Guillame has the inside track, or who might have been listening in on the speakerphone.

"That's your position, Teddi?"

"Absolutely, Hans. I've done nothing wrong. Nothing," I add emphatically. "I discussed it with a couple of team colleagues, that's all. There are absolutely no grounds for any action against me."

I guess I am warning him, as best I can, that these are tricky waters. But there again, he's probably figured that out by now, and a whole lot more besides. Interesting that he is querying the change. Brett can't have aligned Hans with the change before speaking with me. And since Hans appears to be speaking to me before Brett, then does that mean that Hans trusts me ahead of Brett? Could he be about to rebuff the proposal? Or just testing my resolve?

"Teddi, I need to understand this further," he muses. You're not kidding, I think. And how.

"Don't take any action in response to what Brett has said. If HR get in touch, refer them to me, would you? I think we need to elevate this discussion to the correct level."

"That's fine Hans. To be honest, it seems such a fantastical situation I can't help but believe that there must be some way of sorting out all of this."

"Agreed." He pauses. "Right, I can see that you haven't had your morning coffee yet, and we know how you like that. Leave it with me. It may be next week before I get back to you, ok?"

"Sure," I reply, as we walk out of my office together. Hans heads back down the corridor to his office, I head over to Em's office.

"Em, I'm just grabbing a coffee from the kitchen. Want one?"

"Sorry, Teddi just about to head into a meeting. Still on for tonight?"

"Definitely. Something for you to mull over though between now and then, though." I pause, before plunging ahead. "I'm joining the ranks of the imminent departees."

I can see her start.

"What? That's insane. We need to talk, swap updates urgently," she counters.

"Too right. See you at six-ish in the lobby?"

"Diarised. See you then, Teddi."

Chapter 43

"Teddi? Dieter Spielman. Could I have ten minutes of your time?"

I've wandered back from the kitchen with two coffees. Somehow this seems like one of those times when the first coffee of the day will barely touch the sides, and I can't be fagged to go back to the kitchen in short order. I've barely sat down at my desk when a cadaver walks into my office.

That's not strictly true, of course. A corpse hasn't really walked into my office. This isn't some 1950's zombie B-movie, but it's how I'm feeling, and this Dieter guy looks like shit, emanating gloom and menace in equal measure. I could swear that the room has suddenly darkened.

He sits down opposite me. Clearly this isn't a request: I'm fighting the urge to remind him that it is.

"Dieter. I don't believe that we have met before. Which department are you from?"

"Teddi, I lead the head office HR team."

Interesting. I could have sworn I met the Head of HR when I arrived here. I decide to play this nice and polite and professional.

"A delight to meet you, Dieter. I haven't seen you around before?"

"I tend not to get involved in the day to day minutiae. My focus is on strategy and risk management, and the HR needs of the Board."

"Sounds wonderful, Dieter. How can I help you?"

He flexes his hands, and smiles. Well, I say he smiles, but it's more like Dracula bearing his fangs in the moments before sinking them into your jugular.

"Well, Teddi, it's less a case of how you can help me, and more how I can help you with your redeployment."

"My redeployment?"

"Come now, Teddi, I believe that Brett has already discussed this with you?"

"Brett mentioned something, *Dieter*, but Brett isn't my line manager, Hans is."

"You aren't going to be awkward about this, are you *Teddi*?"

"Awkward? Professionalism is my watchword in all matters, *Dieter*." We are emphasizing one another's names, subtly, but clearly. This is like some rapiers-at-dawn fencing duel, not a meeting in an office in the 21st century. But at least I now know who, or rather what, he is: one of those death's-head types that HR wheel out when nasty work has to be done. Not the nice and smiley twenty- something girls who interview you, or welcome you to your new job, but the hatchet man you never see unless the shit is hitting the fan.

I continue.

"The point is that I have discussed Brett's views with Hans, and Hans would like you to take this directly up with him."

"But you agree with the change, of course."

"Dieter, as and when Hans and I discuss my career, we will formulate a way forward and then I'll have something to agree to. In the interim, I suggest that you discuss any *ideas* or *views* that you may have with Hans, as he requests."

He looks at me, struggles to control a twitch, then rises and walks out of the room.

He hasn't even ended the meeting. No goodbye, no handshake. Nothing.

I get up and walk to the door, watch him stride down the corridor towards Hans' office. I could swear that the lights briefly dim as he passes.

The dark prince of night.

Where do they get these people from?

Chapter 44

What a morning. It's barely nine am, and things are moving bloodily fast. I feel like I've been in the boxing ring and squared up for a title fight, before even starting email. And my To Do list is right out the window. I know that one day I'll look back at these events and describe them as character building, even though I've quite enough character already, thank you very kindly. I'll probably add, with a wise yet wry smile, "After all, what doesn't kill you can only make you stronger." Right now, though, I have to call them as they are, which is shitty.

The office instant coffee really isn't reaching the spot. I leave my suit jacket on my chair back, tuck my wallet and phone into my meeting folio, leave my office door open and head out to my favourite coffee shop. I need to make some calls, and my office is like Grand Central Station at six pm on a Friday. Noisy, busy and you can't hear yourself think.

I leave a message for Arlene. "Hey Arlene, Teddi Woods. Wonder if I can discuss the US share exchange protocol with you at some point? I'm free at 2 o'clock if that would work for you."

She's smart, and will realize immediately that what I am actually telling her is that our conference call with Tad is off, but that we do need to talk, but to anyone listening in it's just a normal business exchange.

Then I pound the pavements to the coffee shop. I love walking. Like swimming, or running, the steady rhythm of walking is calming, allowing my brain to relax, recharge and, oftentimes, come up with some great insights.

It seems fairly clear now that Brett has HR in his pockets, and the project team bullied into line, but it doesn't look like Hans is as yet on message.

Hans has a great reputation in the business, but he hasn't been overly communicative with me whilst I have been here. In fact, I have felt dumped in the deep end in a role that has proven itself to be both isolating and isolated, and I've been grateful for the little support and camaraderie I've found with Arlene and Tad.

Early on in this deal I sat down with Hans to ask for hints and tips, suggestions and ideas, so that I could steal a march on Wildcat. After all, Hans had the reputation of being a vast store of knowledge and experience. The conversation had been less than illuminating, however. He'd been surprisingly reticent, outlining the bare bones of a deal he had completed a couple of years before but without indicating the planning used. It had left me wondering whether there was any substance, maybe he didn't have as much experience as suggested.

Since then, and as I got to spend time in the office, I'd realized he worked prodigious hours. In meetings he produced quality thought, and day in and day out he was continually guiding disparate arms of the business. He always seemed there for the Board, steadying them when the shit hit the fan, pulling rabbits out of hats for ideas and solutions. Plus he seemed to have the knack of knowing the issues that might crop up, before they did, and directing activity around what could have been obstacles.

I had begun to wonder what the business would be like if he didn't do all of this, and whether his lack of time for my area was less a reluctance to work with me and more a reflection of the absolute and unutterable demands on his time elsewhere. Maybe he let me get on with things, even made me, because he trusted me? It would certainly explain a lot.

But this is all fine and dandy, I think as I walk the pavement. The test of this is at hand, and I need Hans and Guillame to find a way forward. On the Board and their bonus. On the changed paper. Crikey, on my career.

For the first time since arriving in Geneva I feel anxious, no longer reassured. No longer part of an exciting whole, but somehow separate and unwanted. Geneva suddenly no longer feels like home, or a friend, and I wonder where I belong.

I shake myself as I walk. This isn't Geneva's fault. It isn't Switzerland's. The Bretts of this world are everywhere, and they will play their games wherever and everywhere. I can't control what Brett does, I tell myself, but I can control how I respond, and alienation and despondency aren't the way forward. A dangerous thing, alienation – a little can breed a whole self-fulfilling prophecy of doom. I've taken the fight back to Brett internally in the office, time now I took the next step and controlled the external situation.

The coffee shop is humming and, black coffee in hand, I retire to a discreet nook and settle down to the task at hand – calling old contacts at headhunters in London, and finding new ones in Geneva. Maybe neither Christoph nor Hans want me to look for another job, or at least maybe Christoph doesn't want me to leave Geneva, but there is no guarantee right now that Hans and Guillame will win the day (or even if they do, that my role will be safe). I need to protect number one.

I need to create a storm of interest around my CV, so I start calling my London contacts, making arrangements to send them my CV and sit down with them in a couple of weeks' time. Christoph and I are heading back to the UK for a friends' wedding on the Saturday, so I decide to head back a couple of days earlier and spend the time meeting with my contacts, discussing the market and the attractiveness of my Geneva stint to a UK buyer. We'll agree the way forward, and if all goes to plan, they will start putting me on their long and short lists, the ensuing flurry of interviews will increase the appetite of prospective employers, and I should land a role within the next month or three.

That's the way the market usually works, anyway.

Geneva is slightly different. I don't just need to make contact with the headhunters, I need to find out who they are and persuade them that I am their perfect candidate. Each meeting with them will be a job interview in of itself, two hours of putting myself forward and jumping through hoops like a showjumping pony. None of the meetings are to be taken lightly, but the ones with a stone cold contact, who has to be warmed up, are always the hardest.

So I spend the next two hours calling, talking and arranging meetings in both locations, then head back to the office. This time I walk purposefully. Geneva feels like my friend again.

Chapter 45

If the day started crazy, like a brawl in a bar, the afternoon saw me relentlessly pile drive through the day's urgent tasks.

The call with Arlene had been short but sweet and providing a rare moment of humanity in an otherwise brutal day. She'd been sagacious about Tad, and his sudden promotion and move to Malaysia. "Happened before, Teddi, and it'll happen again. Can't blame the guy. Let's give him a couple of weeks to settle in then get in touch, let him know we still think of him as a friend. Keep the door open, you know?"

But she had sounded stunned about my run in with Brett. It didn't sound like the news had reached her, and she soon confessed why.

"Teddi, after we talked, I realized that this was way over my head, and way too big to cope with on my own. This just wasn't what we were hired to handle. So I took myself off to the Executive Floor over here determined to wrangle myself some time with someone senior in whom I could confide and with whom I could consult. I found the Americas Finance Director - Rod Corbett, you know him? After I explained it to him, he immediately dragged me into the MD's office, and I went through the whole story again."

"What was their reaction?"

"Absolutely stunned, Teddi, they seemed absolutely stunned. At a guess, the MD was part of the team, like Guillame, who voted the bonus scheme down. You said Guillame looked shocked when you mentioned it that time at the airport? Anyway, they said they would look into it, and no-one mentioned a job change or loss. You know what, though?"

"What?"

"It felt good to explain what we had discovered. I felt relieved, Teddi, and when I went home, for the first time in weeks I got a full night's sleep."

"Maybe we should have discussed this with more people, and earlier, Arlene."

"Maybe. But there again, until very recently we had no idea what we were dealing with, right?"

"True, but was it our burden to carry alone?"

"Who could we have approached? Doesn't sound like the rest of the Kingdom team have a pair together."

We laugh.

"Maybe the people we have just spoken to?"

"Ah, maybe. But don't forget, at the start, we didn't know who was in on this."

"True, Teddi, very true."

"Easy for us to say that after the fact, right? Look, Arlene, just so you know, I am starting to look externally for a role. It sounds like this could yet turn around and turn out good, but there are a lot of unknowables. It's not something that I particularly want to do, but I have to have a Plan B, you know?"

"Teddi, in your shoes I would do the same thing. You have to look after your interests."

"Been a privilege working with you though, Arlene."

"You too, Teddi, and if you need a reference, I'd

be more than happy to provide one."

Which is when the day stops. We could have ended the conversation agreeing to stay in touch whatever happened, but to offer to supply a reference is to offer to put yourself under an obligation to that person. It's a serious offer to stay in touch, more meaningful than blasé agreements to "do lunch sometime", or "grab a coffee when you're next in town", and we both know it. I am blown away by her generosity.

"Teddi?"

"Sorry Arlene, I was momentarily silenced by your offer, because it was sincerely meant, and I am really honoured by it. Thank you. I would be delighted if you would act as a referee for me."

"My pleasure, Teddi."

After which we discuss what could be in it, and agree to talk again in a week, unless something happens before then that we need to evaluate jointly. As I put down the phone I recognize, not for the first time, that in Arlene I have a friend for the long haul.

Chapter 46

"Time to go, Teddi. You ready?"

It's Em. She's at the door, grinning from ear to ear, and with horror I realize that, no, I'm not ready, not even close. My To Do list isn't ready for Monday morning, my laptop and files need putting away, and don't get me started on my make up.

"Get a move on, sister. We have some serious socialising to do."

I can't help but grin back. Her energy is infectious. Time to dump everything in the cupboards, dolly myself up, and head on out. Fifteen minutes later we are walking out of the lobby into the early evening sunshine. We head to our favourite watering hole. Geneva can be a little staid sometimes, but even so there are places you can head to for relaxation, in style, and at a price, it has to be said. You do have to reserve ahead, though.

"Kir royale?"

"You know me too well. Unless you have any other ideas?"

"They stock your favourite sauvignon blanc?"

"Yeah, but it's an import, and you'd think you were drinking liquid gold the prices they charge. I'd rather go local. What about the ones from Christoph's parents vineyard?"

She reappears with a wine bucket and two

glasses, and we settle into a window seat.

"Cheers."

"Proost."

We each attack our glass.

"I needed that. What a day."

"Tell me about it."

"Will do, but you need to spill the beans first. What *is* going on?"

"What is going on? The million dollar question. Where to start."

I lean in, and lower my voice to a whisper so that she can barely hear me and is obliged to lean in too. Don't want anyone else hearing this.

"How about me and two others stumbling on a plan by the Board to close a factory just so that they will get a bigger bonus? How about a scheme by the project lead to get all three of us out of the way, with me heading home in short order and one of the others already posted rapidly overseas?"

Her jaw has dropped.

"How about the fact that not all the Board know that they should actually have been dealing with a recommendation to close a different plant, and have been hoodwinked? How about Hans, Guillame and goodness knows who else fighting it out at this very moment? How about yours truly looking rapidly for another job?"

"Holy shit, Teddi. You have got to be kidding me."

"Not even slightly."

"But that's…"

"Don't even try to articulate what is on your mind right now. Trust me when I say you are best well out of this one."

"But this can't happen, Teddi. It's a scandal."

"You know it. I know it."

"Surely this will get sorted out?"

"Will the Board alter the way the bonus plan works, even if it changes the factory affected by the decision? Will the culpable Board members go? Will they go quietly? Will they shoot the messenger? You would hope that the best interest of the business and shareholders is to see change, right?"

"Sure."

She looks at me and thoughtfully takes a sip of wine.

"Start from the top?"

"Start from the top."

So I do, still sotto voce, from the day the two emails came through, via Arlene, Tad, Guillame, London, Geneva, Brett, Hans and Dieter, stopping only to refill glasses and attempt to empty them.

"So that is where we are at as of right now. Lot to take in, right? Look, I'm heading to the bar to get another bottle, give you a moment to absorb everything."

I return with the wine, a large pitcher of water, and a suggestion that we order something to eat before the wine goes to our heads and we keel over, hammered.

We are looking through the menu when she murmurs what is on her mind.

"Teddi, the only project in the office involving a factory closure right now is the project that Brett is leading. So far, though, you're the only head office casualty. Why is that?"

"Don't know, truth be told. In theory any one of the team who saw both emails could join the dots. Don't know why I am the target, really don't."

"Here's the thing. Last year, I worked with Brett on the bond financing, if you remember?"

"Yup, remember it well. He came out of that covered in glory, didn't he?"

"He did. The thing is, something happened on the project that I never could understand at the time."

I wait for her to continue.

"We were progressing well in talks with a consortium of banks, getting all of the detail ironed out and very close to signature, when he suddenly switched the focus to one bank only. Suddenly, we were getting financing from only one supplier, but the terms didn't just stay the same, they got better. Even though one bank was now carrying all of the risk. The deal hurtled through the Board, and I have to say that the financing did come on line very quickly. It was a very good outturn by Brett and no mistake. It's just that I've never been able to understand how we were able to switch to just one debt provider and on such good terms."

She takes a sip of water.

"But then I talk to you, and I realize that the bank involved in the bond financing was also the bank that advised the Board on their bonus scheme."

Crikey.

"Surely they would have Chinese walls in place, Em. Surely they have scrupulous separateness between different parts of the bank?"

"But what if they didn't, Teddi? What is this is all connected? Maybe they get additional fees depending on how the bonus scheme performs? What do we conclude then?"

What indeed? It's a monstrous conclusion, and I say so.

"Em, if that is the case, then this is even more scandalous than I thought. Thinking about it, though, what is in it for Brett? Why would he do this? OK, Armand I can see benefitting from the bonus pump, but Brett? Surely it's all downside for him?"

She looks at me and shrugs. Neither of us wants to say anything out loud, but horrendous conclusions dangle before our eyes. A Board hoodwinked by the few. The few corrupted absolutely by greed. Facilitation payments, backhanders, and all sorts of illegal and immoral cash flows. I feel sick.

But then another thought occurs to me.

"And that is why both you and I are being forced out of head office in very short order. Not only do we each know a great deal, but we know each other, and if we ever were to get together and share our insights, then the link between the deal last year and the scandal this would be exposed. Armand and Brett are the connection, and that's why we're being forced out. They're terrified of you and I doing exactly what we are doing right now, and Brett is doing his damnedest to prevent it."

Chapter 47

For what seems like an eternity, we stare at each other. She cracks first, and bursts into gales of laughter. I can't help it, can't resist the need to break the tension, and join in. We dissolve into hysterics, unable to control ourselves.

People stare. I'm trying to avoid meetings her gaze, but every time I look up at her, she's looking at me. I'm weak with laughter, nearly weeing myself, and wriggling in my seat.

"Oh, please, stop. Look away. I can't cope."

And she is as bad. We need a few moments to calm ourselves down before she can reply.

"Teddi, that cannot be it. Tell me that that isn't it. Tell me we aren't losing our jobs just because some loser is shitting himself."

"I know, trust me, I know. If it wasn't so serious it would be pathetic. Our entire lives are being turned upside down, and for what? Dear grief, Em, you couldn't make it up."

We "hoo" with stiffled giggles a bit more until we calm again, and can continue our conversation quietly and discreetly, as before.

"We haven't made a mistake, have we?" she asks.

"Well, there could be other links, but you and I are the only ones moving. There has been no formal restructuring announcement. And both changes are unduly hasty. There *is* one upside, though."

"There is?"

"Sure. He's taken his best shot already. Played his cards. I mean, we are already at the end of a barrel."

"Puts us in a good position now, you mean?"

"Bang on."

"I'll drink to that," she replies, and we raise our glasses.

"Do you know, Em, I thought I'd be angry but I'm not. I'm relieved, you know? Suddenly all of the mystery disappears and the whole situation becomes a lot more manageable."

"Couldn't agree more."

"What do we do now, though? How do we take this forward?"

"There's something you need to know, Teddi."

Oooer. I wait for her to continue.

"You know how I'm due to head back home at the end of the month? Well, you may or may not know that my father works for one of our competitors?"

"I know the CEO has your surname. You're not saying that he is your dad?"

"That's exactly what I am saying. I didn't want to join them because I just thought that everyone would think that any success of mine was due to who my father was, and nothing to do with my own capabilities and my own efforts. So I joined this business, and until this point I thought that was a good idea."

She takes another sip of wine.

"Anyway, to get to the point. When I told him what was happening here, he was shocked. Called me back the same day and told me to call someone there, gave me a name and contact details. I did that, I've had a Skype interview today and basically I've accepted an offer of employment from them. I handed in my resignation today, subject to references, just before I left the office."

Wow, that's a turn up for the books and no mistake.

"Crikey."

"Indeed."

"Hats off to you. Way to go. Very pleased for you."

"Thanks," she smiles. "I'm feeling good about it."

"You should," I reply. "Seriously, that is very cool. I mean, why not? Don't you have some form of non-compete in your contract, though? I know I do."

"Sure, six months. I've decided to kill the time volunteering. I'll be teaching school children in Latin America for most of it."

"Making constructive use of the time, in other words?"

"Right on. But what will *you* do, Teddi?"

"Only one thing left open to me now, I guess. A short message for Guillame and Hans, suggesting that a possible connection between the two events has occurred to me. Maybe to us? That and accelerate the job hunt."

"Want me to mention you to Dad, see what's possible on their side of the street? I mean, what do you have to lose now?"

What indeed?

"OK, go for it."

"Excellent. That's just what I expected from you Teddi, a decisive attitude and can-do spirit."

"You're too kind" I smile to her.

"Look. You and I know one another well by now. I know what you're like to work alongside and I know what Hans is losing if he lets Brett get away with this. If nothing else, it will keep your options open and your confidence up, right?"

"Right."

"By the way," she adds. "When you leave those messages, you can say that the idea occurred to us in conversation this evening. If those two guys are on the level, and are even half as intelligent as we think they are, the connection between the two activities and our departures will also occur to them."

"And that we've spotted that."

She nods.

"I don't think they will need an excuse to go for Brett, but organisations have a funny way of dealing with things. Brett could lose his job for targeting us, rather than this scandal with the Board decisions and the bank."

"Way more discreet."

"Exactly."

"Though I wonder what would happen with Armand," I add. "OK, I'll do that."

She puts down her glass, as I do mine. Our sharing platter of antipasti has arrived, and we tuck in. Parma ham, artichokes, sun-roasted tomatoes, bread, oven-baked garlic, grilled aubergine, bresaola and salami are just what we need right now. I'm feeling ravenous, am probably tipsy, and attack both food and mineral water with equal intensity.

"You know, Em," I muse, after quite some time has passed. "When we came out tonight I had no idea the evening would turn out quite like this."

"You mean, that we would solve a mystery?"

"Something like that. Amazing, isn't it, how a major drama in your life can suddenly straighten itself out."

“Fate, Teddi,” she comments, succinctly.
“Isn’t it just.”
And I have to agree.

Chapter 48

We've demolished a delicate plate of red mullet, and are nursing black coffees. We're both a lot more mellow, now, the mellowness that comes from good food, good wine, and, if it can be admitted, from a sense of pressure eased.

"Teddi, there is one thing that amazes me in all of this."

"Only one?"

"I don't mean about the two matters we have been discussing. What amazes me is that even when you've been in the middle of extremely testing circumstances, you've still kept on pushing forward. Take the lunch with Guillame. He's telling you there are major changes ahead, big risks, and instead of meekly shutting up and taking the blows you take the moral high road and decide to beard him about some crazy idea you've had to solve the global economic crisis. That's insane. Big, beautiful but insane."

"Thank you, I suppose. Didn't particularly feel like that at the time," I shrug. "Anyway, there must be others coming up with the same idea, somewhere in the world."

"First I have heard of it, not seen it in the financial press" she replies. "What did Guillame say?"

"Something similar," I respond. "But the views

of two people aren't exactly a comprehensive survey, right."

She laughs. "True," she adds. "But let's change the subject. What does Christoph make of all of this?"

"Very supportive, lots of advice, big hugs."

"And if you return to the UK?"

She's hit the nail on the head.

"I don't really know. Put it another way, he says he loves me. He spends vast amounts of time with me. He's introduced me to his parents. He gives great advice, is a shoulder to lean on, and is my best friend. Great, right? But, and here is the but and it's a big one, we have been seeing each other for nearly a year and a half, and there has been absolutely no hint of him popping the question."

"Ah" is all she needs to say in reply. Just like Immy and Issy, Em is firmly of the view that if a guy is going to propose, he will usually do that between twelve and eighteen months after starting dating. Beyond that, the chances reduce to virtually zero. Sure, there are those rare cases where people end up marrying after five or ten years, but more commonly it's the other way around.

"And the sixty four thousand dollar question is, even if there were no traumas on the job front, would I break up with him, anyway? So, would I be heading back to the UK anyway? In which case, is this all just fortuitous timing? And you know what? I have no idea? I love Christoph, beyond all reason, he's the love of my life. Certainly don't want to break up with him, but am I just hanging around, treading water, instead of getting on with my life? Wish I knew..."

"And talking about it with Christoph?"

"Is scary. After all, if he says he never will ask,

then what do I do?"

"Maybe you're there, anyway? Procrastinating just puts off the dreaded day…"

She is correct, of course.

"I know, I know. Won't be tonight. But you're right, the 'big conversation' will be happening soon. I'll just have to pick my time…"

"Just don't leave it weeks or months."

"I won't," I laugh in reply. "Anyway, I'm heading to the UK for interviews in a couple of weeks, which I'll have to tell him about as it is just before a wedding that we're going to together. He'll wonder why I am going early to the UK."

"Isn't he taking you to his parents for the weekend sometime in August, for your birthday?"

"Mmmn, yes. Take your point, when do I talk to him? Do I talk with him before I head to the UK? After the wedding but before seeing his parents? Could be awful timing in any scenario."

I could do without this. But life has a habit of presenting up with unavoidable events, and I'm learning fast that it's how you respond that counts.

Chapter 49

"Anyway, that's my life dissected," I reply. "What's going on with you and the mystery guy you've been seeing?" I'm trying gamely to change the subject, and she plays ball.

"All over."

Crikey, even for Em this is a brutally frank reply. No meandering around the subject, approaching it obliquely, or hedging the response with subtleties. I look closely at her. Her talk is nonchalant, but her shoulders slope, her back curves and the smile doesn't quite reach her eyes, which suddenly seem wide, dark and sad. I suddenly realize that she wanted me to change the subject, maybe even worked the conversation as she has so that it would get around to this. I've been a self-obsessed klutz. All of those supportive comments, even a compliment; all the time she was hurting and hoping that we would eventually get around to supporting her, that it would be her turn.

"Why don't you start at the beginning?" I suggest, as gently as possible.

She looks at me, a shadow passing briefly over her face.

"The short version is that I saw him for six months, and then I broke things off earlier this week, same day my move back to The Netherlands was announced. It would never have continued after a move, wouldn't have been possible, so it seemed the only route forward."

"Well that explains your comment earlier about not putting off romantic decisions. But what about all of those romantic trysts, dinners, nights away? Couldn't you have continued, at least until things became formal? I thought you were besotted with this guy?"

"Were?" she replies, slightly sharply. "Still am, Teddi, and think I will be for some time yet. Don't think other guys are going to get a look in any time soon."

I wait. There is clearly more to this than she is telling, but I decide to see if silence will help her open up. Certainly too many direct questions could well have the opposite effect.

At length, she takes a deep breath, then replies.

"He's married, you know. Did I ever tell you that?"

She shrugs, looking ever more lost, but I struggle not to recoil, or at least show my shock.

"It's ok," she adds. "I wasn't expecting you to support adultery, my being the *other woman*. If it makes any difference, it wasn't planned, I didn't set out for this to happen."

She pauses and looks at me. I stay silent, waiting for more to unfold, but hoping, a little embarrassingly, that I wouldn't be called on to support this.

"I guess I was flattered, I thought it was innocent, just business. When it progressed, I thought it was meaningless, fun, that I could handle it. But it doesn't work like that, does, it? The human heart I mean? I came to realize that I was falling in love, and at the same time noticed how he was always missing when I needed him.

We had our, what do you call it, big conversation? He would never leave his wife, didn't want to prejudice his job. Don't look at me like that. Yes, I know that these are the same old stories, the same old replies, used by adulterers for hundreds of years. And yes, I should have known better. Thing is, I think I did. It's why I insisted on the conversation in the first place."

Her shoulders sag again.

"So what you're saying is that your move back home to The Netherlands is a red herring? That this would have happened anyway? Maybe it just accelerated it?"

"Something like that."

"Then congratulations, Em. For having the balls and commonsense to get your shit together. For getting back your self-esteem. And for opening yourself up to a real future."

I raise my glass, she does too, to her credit (a sure sign she will get over all of this, in time).

"Aren't you at all curious, Teddi? Don't you want to know who it was? My mystery man?"

"Sorry to disappoint, but I can't say I am. I mean, are you telling me it's someone from the office? That's a rhetorical question, by the way. Middle-aged guy having a midlife crisis and relieving his youth via an affair is not exactly news, but there is a difference between knowing that guys could do this in general, and that one has done it in particular. I don't want to look at some guy on Monday morning in a meeting knowing he is 'the one for Em.' I'll lose all respect for the guy."

"That's very stoic."

"Not really. When I started work after leaving University, I worked in a large team that included two very different women. One kept her business life and personal life very separate. The other had numerous office flirtations. The first was seen as a real tough bitch by the guys, the latter as great fun. They both got promoted, but the first was promoted faster and further than the second. They both left, though it was the second one who left earlier."

"And the relevance, Teddi?" Em seems a little surprised.

"The relevance? Well, I'm not sure that a woman can 'have it all.' Did the first one have it right? She kept her romantic life out of the office and firmly at home. She used the business to get what she could to boost her CV, but didn't identify too closely with the environment, so moving on was ok and office machinations didn't damage her self-esteem. The second was more in touch with her emotional self, so you'd guess that in later life she'll be the happier one, more fulfilled. But dating married guys is self-defeating, the worst of both worlds, Em. Keep romance out of the office environment, or recognize that it's where you're likely to meet your life partner, but whatever you do, avoid married men. A terrible waste of love and youth and all its gifts."

I pause.

"Shit, sorry, I'm pontificating. Point is this. You're worth far more than being on the scrag end of some guys' spare time and spare emotions. Look for someone who is looking for someone like you in their life, and don't look anywhere else. Sorry if I sound hacked off. I'm not hacked off with you, but with anyone who just wants to use you. You deserve far better. Far better."

She smiles, slowly. This time it reaches her eyes.

"Thanks Teddi. I needed that," she adds with a

self-deprecating laugh. She knows I'm not condoning what she's been up to, but offering her some emotional support.

"You know the real irony about this?"

"No?"

"You'll get back to The Netherlands, be pushing forward with your life, and then suddenly, when you're least looking for it, love will walk into your life. Honest to God, it will. Six months from now you'll be dating some guy and never have been happier."

"Right," she laughs again. But she is clearly tickled by the notion, and we sketch a series of increasingly daft scenarios about how this would play out. She is laughing, relaxing, and letting out the tension.

Chapter 50

"Night, Em, it's been lovely to see you again."

"You too, Teddi. I'm going to miss our coffees, but I really do want you to stay in touch and come visit me, whatever happens with jobs and guys."

"I will, Em, I will. You're a good friend, and I'd hate to lose our friendship."

Em and I have called it a night, and we're stood outside the restaurant, saying our farewells to the evening, but also foreshadowing our imminent departures from Geneva. We're also a bit tiddly, which is maybe contributing.

She has called a cab, I've called Christoph (who had offered to come and collect me), and we hug huge goodbyes as her car arrives. It pulls just beyond where we are standing, so she runs forward, and as she runs forward, and just for a moment, I get the fleeting impression that the car isn't empty. Just for a moment, there is a movement, as if someone inside were shifting position.

It can't be *him*, I think. Surely that is over? And then it filters into my (admittedly boozed) brain that there was something familiar about the shadow that moved inside the car. But, my brain *is* boozed, and I'm still standing there, thinking through lead, when Christoph pulls up at the kerb.

"Hey there, Teddi-Bear. How was the big night

out?"

Christoph is smiling, hugely.

"Wow, thanks," I reply and kiss him. He kisses me back. It's like we've just met for a hot date, maybe three months into a relationship. He pulls me to him, and hugs me tightly, crushing me against him. He's clearly pleased to see me. Time we went home...

It's nearly two am before we finally lie in one another's arms, blissed and sated. Then it hits me, a blast of clarity and realization, obliterating all before it.

"Guillame!"

Chapter 51

"What? What is it, Teddi-Bear?" Christoph asks groggily. He must've already been asleep.

"Nothing. It can wait until morning."

"It woke you up, but can wait until morning?" He doesn't sound convinced. "What's on your mind? C'mon Teddi, tell me."

At which I crumple, all the tension of the last day or two overwhelming me, and through tears of relief I run through the entire evening's events.

"So you're saying that I arrived before you could fully process what you had seen in the car, but now you know?"

"Mmmn. There was something familiar that I couldn't quite place. But it just hit me. In the park (remember how Guillame and I went for a walk on Thursday?) we sat on a bench and I merrily expounded on my solution to the global economic crisis. Well, as I talked, Guillame criss-crossed his legs as he relaxed back against the bench, and it was that movement, that criss-cross of legs, that I saw in the car."

"A criss-cross of legs?" He sounds slightly incredulous.

"I know, I know, hardly definitive proof, right? But it was so exact a match, so precisely similar…" My voice trails off.

"Perhaps a sub-conscious mannerism of his?

You know that it is virtually impossible for a person to control all of their body language at the same time? Maybe he does it when he is with a woman he is attracted to?"

"Or maybe when he is under stress, in a situation he can't control, or perhaps when he is hiding something? A hint that something is being covered up?"

I ignore the jibe, though. We're both tired and it's just not worthy of him. On one level there is a compliment – Christoph is jealous, wants me for himself – and I feel a brief warmth of pleasure, but I'm not the sort of person to provoke that kind of reaction deliberately, nor play to it.

"And what have you been hiding, Teddi?" is his response.

What? What on earth is he talking about?

"Hunting for jobs in the UK? Arranging to fly back there for interviews before Issy's wedding and your birthday weekend in Vaudois?"

Ah, so that's it. It's three am, and without planning it we're in the middle of 'the big conversation.' His questions are pointed but careful, hanging in the air like a quiver of arrows. He's got a right to be annoyed, but I hadn't wanted the discussion to take place like this. Clearly we aren't going back to sleep any time soon, and if I don't sort this out soon, the evening could yet descend into an all-out argument.

I take a deep breath.

"Christoph, it's like we said. I love being here in Switzerland, but two days ago my life was turned upside down. I don't know how my work situation will pan out. I mean, I could be back in the UK within a month. I could even be back in the UK and out of work. So I've made contact with headhunters both here in Geneva and back in

London, and I'm trying to work up some excitement around my CV to create some options."

He looks pained.

"And us, Teddi, how do we fit into all of this?"

"Christoph, this isn't meant to harm us in any way. I didn't start this situation, remember? But I do have to find some options."

He continues to look at me. There are no obvious signs of anger, or coldness, but equally he is controlling his emotions. I don't know how to interpret this. I've never seen him angry. Maybe this is the start?

"I meant, couldn't we have discussed options together?"

My shoulders sag with relief.

"Of course. I meant to raise this all today. I mean today at a rational hour, not today at 3am. Just got overtaken by events. I'm sorry Christoph. I didn't mean to upset you. I love you, maybe more than you know. But what could our options be? Would you suggest I move in with you until I get a job? I don't want us to live together (I wouldn't even live together whilst engaged) – you know me, I'm very old-fashioned like that. So what could feasibly be the options? For sure, it would be different if we were married, but we aren't. I mean, is this relationship going to develop to the next level, or am I treading water?"

Not for the first time this evening, my voice trails away again, but there it is, the bogey subject is out on the table. There's an element of relief in this, but more than that I feel sad. Unutterably, vomitingly sad. I don't want this to end, but somehow the end seems to be looming.

"I'm sorry Christoph. Sorry I've been such a lousy communicator over the last couple of days. You're my best friend, you know? This is all such a mess."

I love him so much it overwhelms me. And I'm making such a mess of things.

He says nothing but pulls me to him. We wrap one another up in warmth. Nothing is resolved, but this is honest. The warmth eases tension, and eventually we fall asleep again, exhausted.

Chapter 52

The next ten days are a blur. Christoph and I go out to dinner and to the theatre. He helps me get my CV super-ready, and prepare to sell myself in interview with the recruiters. We dissect the meetings in Geneva after they take place. We make each other supper after work (work is dull, no-one seems to be around, and I'm steadily working through actions and tasks without any real enthusiasm). We make love (a lot).

But we never discuss the conversation during the early hours of that Saturday morning. Truth be told, so much is going on that I'm secretly pleased we don't - I don't need any more tension in my life right now. And, though it's hard to admit it, Christoph and I feel like we're in a good place. Crazy but true. Life gets shitty, things between us improve. Must be love…

Before I know it, it's time to pack my suitcase for the trip to London. It's barely two weeks since that meeting with Brett, and here I am heading to the UK to look for a job.

It's Wednesday morning. I have a noon flight. Christoph drives me to the airport and we hug goodbye. It's horrible, I don't want to leave, but I have to go. He seems to sense it. He looks into my eyes, pushing a strand of hair back from my face.

"Love you."

“Love you too”

“Knock them out.”

“Will do, promise, Brownies honour.”

“Call me when you land. I worry.”

“I will, I promise. And before I go to sleep.”

He smiles, and I smile back. We don’t want to let go, but I have to head through all of the airport’s security systems and don’t want to miss my flight.

I turn and head through control, but as it turns out traffic is relatively light and I’m in the airline business lounge with time to kill. One of the advantages of all of the business travel meted out by my job over the last couple of years or so is that I’ve accumulated a huge airline reward balance. Plus I have top status. Which means I can get a flight at short notice, and pay for it with rewards. This is cool, it has got to be said, and I wander through the lounge getting a coffee and settling down to read todays papers (that arrived on the red-eye flights this morning). The news is old hat – the app on my phone streams news 24/7 from around the globe – but the commentary is fabulous, and I luxuriate in reading the written word of my native tongue express opinions and debate issues.

I become dimly aware of a hubbub and look up. Passengers are streaming toward the bank of TV screens in one corner of the lounge, jostling to see the screens. This is odd. Wondering what could be going on, I check my news apps – they’re frozen, no update possible.

The area around the screens is crowded now. People break away to make urgent calls. If they’re lucky to get a signal, that is – many are shaking their heads at their phones in evident frustration.

Something *major* has got to be happening, and I

get up to go take a look, unable to resist the pull of crowd excitement.

Getting a good view of a screen with English language coverage takes some doing, I have to jostle for position slightly, but suddenly there it is, a shot of several heads of government. It's some form of news conference happening in real-time.

For a moment or three I can't get to grips with the purpose of the news briefing. The political leader of one of the world's largest economies is commenting about how this move is vital for global security and economic viability. He mentions growth, jobs and ending civil unrest, but so far it's just platitudes, and I can't tell whether he is describing a military coup or appointment of a quango.

Then I see the ticker tape now running across the bottom of the screen, and it all becomes staggeringly clear:

BREAKING NEWS: LEADERS OF "G20Plus" GOVERNMENTS ANNOUNCE GLOBAL ACCORD TO CANCEL DEBT ………………………………………………………

……**BREAKING NEWS**: MULTILATERAL DEBT RELEASE OF ALL DEBT AND BAN ON FURTHER DEBT EXPECTED TO POWER SUSTAINABLE LONG-TERM GROWTH ………………………………………………………

………**BREAKING NEWS**:MULTILATERAL DEBT RELEASE MATCHED WITH GLOBAL REDUCTION IN EXECUTIVE PAY TO 1999 LEVELS ………………………………………………………

............................**BREAKING NEWS:** EURO TO END AS EUROPEAN ECONOMIES BRING BACK THEIR DOMESTIC CURRENCIES ....

........................**BREAKING NEWS:** END TO TAX AVOIDANCE IN SIGHT AS COUNTRIES AGREE A COMMON APPROACH ....

Chapter 53

Holy crap. You're kidding me. This simply cannot be happening. That's what I told Guillame to do to fix things!

I want to yell loudly, protest it was my idea and whoop for joy because I don't care and this is all so fabulous, all at the same time. There's a sudden yawning emptiness in my stomach. I feel sick and impossibly elated, giddy but somehow oddly panicking beneath it all.

I can't have triggered this, can I? Surely someone somewhere had already had the ideas? Formed the ideas? Linked them together?

The screens draw my attention again, and I re-focus my gaze. Now all of the political leaders are in shot, and the announcement is being made. This is clearly a re-run of what has just happened, and an excitable journalist is over talking the speaker and trying to explain the enormity of what has just been let leash upon the globe.

The camera angle is moving to try to frame the full group accurately, and for a moment catches a few hangers-on standing to the right before focusing back in.

That can't be, I think to myself. Surely that wasn't Robert Finch, the guy that Guillame met in London the other week? The one that Tad and Arlene saw open the door?

It's the briefest of glimpses. He's a shadow of an impression, and when the camera angle again catches the group he is nowhere to be seen.

To be honest, one glimpse was enough. He's a fixer, but not a pro-banking lobbyist. Guillame was the link after all, which means my thoughts were used, or at least helped. The excitable journalist doesn't stop talking, and around me people mill, jabbing at their phones, trying to call, email or text. But I don't care. I've seen enough. I know enough, for now at least.

I slip my phone into my pocket, wander over the bar, and slowly make myself a gin and tonic. I return to my seat in a daze, then get back up and wander to the window to stare over the tarmac. It's too enormous a conclusion to take on board, and I stand, stare and sip until the flight is called.

Still dazed, I wander to the gate, automatically shuffling forward in the frequent flyer queue, answering the questions and proffering documents. Phones are switched into flight safe mode, but the flight offers no respite from business class desire to be seen to be *doing something* in response, however irrelevant or futile (when does this kick in? can we re-label our pay? can we re-characterise our debt? the devil will be in the detail.) Around me memos are typed, emails and texts drafted, all for that magic moment when we land at London Heathrow and phones grab a signal again.

I'm feeling removed, at a distance somewhat (and it isn't the additional, on-flight gin and tonic). I mean, I'm probably the only person on the flight to whom this isn't a new idea. And who would I call? Pretty much everyone I know, at some point, has heard me rabbit on about this. My mind drifts back to Geneva, and the furore over the Board paper, and I speculate how this might impact

Armand and Brett.

But it's the wider picture that is most intrigues me now. Are they really sounding the death knell to debt? Are they really getting us off the tightrope walk over the chasm of deferred chaos? How many countries are involved (or not)? If not, surely that government would just act unilaterally anyway?

I wonder how the governments decided to do this and what governments, businesses and people will do with such a lift in financial burdens. Will it bring growth, or drive wars that have been hitherto hindered by the cash squeeze faced by a government? Will the Euro re-emerge again at some point, or will countries currently in the Eurozone see this as the way to escape that permanently and develop real growth (rather than a deflationary, but momentary, boost)? How are countries with huge cash and asset piles, like China, going to react when their power and wealth just dissipate? And what about the retired, who rely on debt assets for income, and for whom this could bring utter penury?

And what about those Board dwellers who will see their income and wealth brought under the real control of shareholders? Will they walk (and if so where to?) Could we see small territories develop packed to the brim with them? And what would *that* be like – differentiation is only possible if there is little competition, not a surfeit?

But somehow it all seems in the lap of the gods, now. Nothing more I can do, and all I want to do is get a signal and call Christoph when we land.

Tomorrow could be interesting, though. The changes could prompt a wave of anxious calls to headhunters. I'm in a prime position to exploit the opportunities, with meetings already booked. But who knows where the positions will open up, as the next few weeks and months go by? Maybe, just maybe, Em and I's positions in Geneva will suddenly firm back up again. If we want them.

I sit back and wait for the tarmac to greet us.

Chapter 54

As the plane hits the tarmac, business class faces the task at hand like gladiators going into battle. Serried ranks, in full suited battle dress, smart phones and tablets held ready to slash, spear and pike.

Everyone switches off flight safe mode as one, and immediately the battle to control bandwidth begins. I grab my hand luggage and race off ahead, only flicking on my phone to call Christoph once near passport control and I have a vague chance of grabbing a bar or three.

"Christoph, it's me. I landed safe and sound."

"Teddi-bear, good. Have you heard?"

"Enough. Stunning isn't it?"

"One way of describing it. What will you do?"

"No idea, barely had time to draw conclusions. Look, I'm just heading through passport control. Can I call you back at the hotel?"

"Of course." A pause. "Darling?"

I know this voice.

"Yes, darling?"

"I love you."

"I love you more."

"I love you most."

And with that we hang up the call. I proffer my passport to the electronic reader, whilst in my pocket my phone bings and pings as it updates for emails, calls and texts. A little while later, ensconced on the Heathrow Express bound for Paddington and my case safely tucked in the rack above my head, I start to run through my messages (scribble pad in hand in order to note actions).

It's worse than I ever expected, but at the same time exactly so. Email after email of 'what ifs' and even one headed 'The devil will be in the detail.' No shit, Sherlock, tell us something we don't know.

None, though, come out and say that the Board pay change is A Good Idea. Not one.

A sweet one from Arlene headed 'Wow' and simply saying 'We gotta talk. Call you tomorrow!' is a welcome change.

I switch it back off. Replying to this tidal wave of facetiousness can wait until I'm back at the hotel, or even tomorrow morning over breakfast.

As I insert my key card into my hotel door, my phone rings. 'Christoph, perfect timing' I think. I pull the phone excitedly out of my pocket but it's Guillame, using his private cell number.

"Teddi Woods."

"Teddi, Guillame….. How are you?"

"Fine. Saw the news. Incredible stuff."

"Incredible indeed. How does it feel to have joined the dots and come up with the idea?"

What? Is he really saying that this is a result of the discussion we had in the park? Blimey!

"Ah well, you know… voiced it, perhaps," I mumble in reply.

I have no idea, really.

"Teddi, can I see you tomorrow morning in my office? Eight am?"

"Guillame, apologies, but I'm in London till the end of the week. Just landed in fact."

There is a pause.

"Teddi, you *have* seen the news?"

"Of course. Multilateral debt release, freeze on any further debt, and a retrenchment on executive pay. End of the Euro as we know it. Caught a chunk of the news conference at Geneva International before I got on the plane."

"That's not all the news, Teddi."

It's not? Nothing on email suggested that there was more news I should be aware of (as if this all wasn't enough.) He interprets my pause correctly.

"We issued a press release after the news conference. Not immediately afterwards, but before markets closed for the day here in Geneva."

"I'll fire up my laptop now Guillame and take a look. Would you like me to call you back once I've read it through?"

"No need Teddi. Take a look when you can but I'll tell you the key news now. The Chairman, Armand, the Group COO and two other Board directors have resigned and will leave with immediate effect. The Supervisory Board (our non-Executives) is to be replaced, in entirety. I'll be the new CEO."

Do what?? What did he just say??

"Quite a change, Teddi," he continues. "And there is more to come. We will be rooting out the greed and complacency that let us to such a state of affairs as you experienced on the Kingdom deal. A new culture for a new focus and a new way forward of engagement with our shareholders, our customers and our suppliers. "

"Congratulations. Sounds amazing, and a lot to do," I venture.

"I'm going to need new people in new roles as well, Teddi," he replies, before adding "which is where you come in."

Ah ha. So now we get to the meat of the call.

"How so?" My tone is cautious.

"Teddi, you alone had the courage to think and act differently to the mindset. Surrounded by greed and fraud at worst and cowardice at best, you ventured to think and act towards the very best ideals. I need that, Teddi. This business needs it. I'm setting up a team to develop new business principles for us, our new ethical code, and roll it out. I want you on board."

Just when I thought the day couldn't get any more astonishing, along comes this.

"That's quite an offer, Guillame. Quite an offer indeed. Can't say it isn't attractive. Thinking around this, you know that one of the features of the executive pay scandal has been how businesses have often had a remuneration officer, charged with regulating executive pay. This person has tended to be someone junior to the people whose pay behaviours they were charged with regulating. I don't want to be in a similar sort of situation: charged with changing that which can refuse to change. It's called 'boxing the problem' and it would just be a waste of effort for everyone if that is all that this is. What plans do you have to ensure that the changes you envisage happen?"

"You would be in charge. You would report directly to me. And delivering this change will be an explicit Board deliverable." he adds. I have a feeling that he is keen to co-opt me, trying to sell me the opportunity. He doesn't totally assuage my concerns. Human beings have a habit of driving their lives toward whatever is in their best interest.

I address this.

"The Board deliverables will have to be couched in terms of delivering what this new team comes up with. If it's the other way around, if individual Board members retain capacity to undermine the will of the Board in either design or implementation, then this will, nevertheless, ultimately fail."

"Understood and agreed, Teddi. So will you take up the challenge?"

My first reaction is to indicate interest but say I'd like to sleep on this before committing. But then I think, why not? This is new, an utterly new way forward for me. I can exit quickly if it turns out to be a disaster. But at the same time this could be the making of me.

"I will. I'd like to get to choose my team, or at least review and veto those I don't want on board. I'd like to do the same for our charter and budget. And I'd like us to be physically located on the same floor as you."

"Very reasonable and understandable requirements, Teddi. Done. Are you happy to leave discussing your pay etc. until you return next week?"

"Well, Guillame, thus far my trust in you has been amply rewarded. So, yes, I'll trust you on this too."

"Excellent. Teddi, I've got things to attend to over the next few days, so if you would excuse me, can we set up a meeting for Monday morning to kick off all of this? Glad to have you on board."

It's as much an order as a request. But it works for me. And he hasn't asked what I am up to over the next few days (though maybe he knows that from Em).

"Of course, Guillame. I'll give Elisabeth, your PA, access to my schedule."

"Thanks, Teddi. See you on Monday."

"See you on Monday, Guillame."

And he hangs up.

Chapter 55

"Good God, Teddi. You cannot be serious."

I've called Christoph as soon as Guillame hung up. My suitcase lies unpacked, my shoes and bag scattered just where they fell as I walked into the room. This is too important to wait a moment longer. I've recounted the conversation as it happened. Pretty much verbatim.

"As I live and breathe, darling."

"So when we spoke at the airport you didn't know about the press release? I thought you were remarkably sanguine…"

I laugh, more than a little embarrassed at my previous sang froide.

"Sorry, Christoph. You must have thought me an oaf. Truth to be told I didn't know, and I was musing on the politicians and their press conference."

"Well that *is* big news. The biggest. The press release from your business is pretty small beer in comparison. But that doesn't alter the importance of your call with Guillame. What do you think of the job?"

"Sounds great. Brilliant."

"You don't sound totally convinced."

"I think I'm just overwhelmed by events."

"Nothing else?"

"No. Well, maybe. It's hard to imagine working

closely with a guy to lead principled change when I know he has had an affair."

"But it ended, right? And if you know this, does it simply make him human? Could anyone live up to the image of a saint that you were carrying around?"

"But I saw him the other night. He was in the car with Em, and they were supposed to have broken up."

"Maybe he just wanted to know what you were up to? Maybe she pleaded for a further chat, and he had to do it to keep her quiet."

"Mmmn, I grant you that," I reply.

We fall silent.

"But it doesn't go the whole way, you know. At the end of the day, he did it, and it gave him lots of practice in duplicity. I mean, there are lots of ways someone can show their humanity without sleeping with someone from the office. I'm still not sure I can trust someone who I know behaves like that, and this role is all about trust."

I'm hoping Christoph is taking my point. "And can I risk my personal reputation by getting involved in some morality agenda if he is capable of being brought down by this?"

Christoph pauses for a short while before he replies.

"Look, Teddi, I agree with you about his personal morals. At the end of the day, a guy stands by his marriage vows or he doesn't. But, maybe the shareholders don't need him to be a monk? Who knows what has been discussed behind closed doors in recent weeks? Maybe he has been open about this, given assurances it won't happen again? Maybe he has come clean to his wife. You can't make assumptions about something like this, Teddi."

"But what about me, what do I do?"

"Well only you can decide what to do about that. Maybe discuss with him on Monday? At a guess, and bearing in mind you think he saw Em one last time the other week, it's very likely that he knows you know. You don't have to be officious about it, but maybe you can agree that you participate as long as that sort of thing doesn't happen. By any Board member."

It's not a bad solution, and I tell him so.

"Are you still going to go ahead with all of your appointments?"

"Good question. I think so. Partly because it would be discourteous to cancel. But partly because of what we have just discussed. It won't harm, and you never know what I will find out along the way about the employment market and its reaction to the news."

"Fair enough," he replies, and with which we turn our call away from the world's dramas and to one another.

Chapter 56

It's a glorious August evening overlooking Lake Geneva, where the Vaudois plateau descends in gently rolling hills to the waterside, through fruit orchards, fields, and vineyards, dotted with castles and country houses, country inns and old burghers' and vintners' houses. It's called La Côte, and its dreamy beauty makes it a hugely popular tourist destination, like Switzerland's own Riviera.

Christoph's family owns a small vineyard, and we are visiting for the weekend to celebrate my birthday with them. We've visited before. They seem to like me. I'm not Swiss, maybe that makes me less than ideal, but his parents have never let on if so, and instead welcome me warmly every time we visit. His mother does insist on calling me by my full name, though. Here I am Theodora.

"Do you know that Theodora means 'Gift of God'?"

"Yes, Chantal, yes I do. It's the reason that my parents gave the name to me."

"But why do you not use this? It is so charming a name."

She's right of course. It *is* charming. But, like all teenagers wanting to fit in I had shortened it to a nickname, something ending in "i", something modern, something like all of my friends. Lexi. Abby. Evie. Rosie. Hollie. Chelsea. Well, they rarely actually ended in "i" but they sounded like they did. So I shortened it and fit right in. Looking back now, I wonder why on earth I did it. I mean, why do so many girls have names ending in "i"? What is that all about, really? Was I really so insecure? Are they?

"Well, Chantal, Teddi seemed more modern, more accessible. And it helped me fit in with my teenage friends."

"But you are not a teenager anymore, Theodora."

"So maybe it is time to reclaim my inheritance, as it were?"

"Well that is a way to describe it. I would say that you are a beautiful and charming woman, why would you not have a beautiful and charming woman's name? Why not embrace the name your parents chose for you?"

So the name stuck.

We've just finished dinner, and Christoph has suggested that we take a walk through the vineyard. He knows that I love doing this. As the sun starts to sink down behind the hills, the lake briefly glitters, and the mountains of the Chablis appellation controlee flare in warmth and brilliance, before descending into shades of cool evening. The dusky sky moves gently from blue through oranges and pinks onto lilacs and purples, before enveloping everything in greys and soft, velvety midnight blue. The rows of vines briefly flare with the setting sun's shades, before merging softly into the background.

I love to stroll through the vineyard, walking up and down the rows as the sun goes down, with glimpses every now and then of the view down to the lake, or maybe up to the hills behind. Christoph has seen this all of his life, but he knows

I love it, and he brings me here each time we visit.

We're walking together, hand in hand, like we have done before, silently, listening to the insects and the birds settle down for the evening and the vines exhale the heat of the day.

Christoph stops, and pulls me to face him.

"You love Switzerland, don't you Teddi?"

"Switzerland? Yes, yes I do. I love being here, love the charm and reserve of the people I meet, love the countryside, the lifestyle, the climate, the quality of life. Perhaps not the influx of hedge funds and billionaires." I look at him. "I love being here with you more than any of that."

"It feels like home?"

"Mmmn, it feels like home, feels right."

He's looking at me, steadily now.

"But what about London? What about your life there? Don't you miss it, don't you want to go back?"

"London? I miss my friends, but we have IM, texts, Skype and we can visit each other whenever we want. I miss my parents, but they can too, I mean, I even managed to get them onto Skype last time I saw them, they're real silver surfers now. London is wonderful, but it will continue to be there, and I can visit it again any time. Home is where you want it to be."

"And your apartment?"

"A nest egg."

"But what about your job situation here? This new role working for Guillame? Do you like the role? Do you even want it? Is it you?"

"Well, it's true I didn't envisage taking on the role of ethics arbiter," I reply with more than a modicum of truth. "I'm not too sure about it in the longer term, where it will lead, you know."

"Well, you could always run with it for a year or

two, get the business into the position where it has a set of principles, people are trained, that sort of thing, then maybe take a professorship in Business Ethics. The elite universities will queue up for someone with your knowledge and insight, you know. My suggestion is you run with it for a year or two, then see where you want to take your life after that."

At which point it hits me like a sledgehammer to my solar plexus, so hard I'm momentarily winded.

A few weeks ago, the day Em told me she was being shipped back to The Netherlands, Christoph dragged me out for supper. We were walking along to the restaurant, talking about all that had happened that day, and had casually window-shopped the upmarket boutiques. Christoph had drawn us to a halt in front of a jewellers' store.

"Fabulous jewels, Teddi."

"You aren't kidding. Gorgeous," I'd said, a little distractedly.

"Which are your favourites?"

We were looking at a window display of all sorts of pieces, and all sorts of stones.

"I like the diamonds, but I don't like the ones that flash multi-colours, you know, blue, pink, yellow all at the same time. They seem garish, somehow. Diamonds go with anything, but preferably in a platinum setting. Yellow gold clashes, is a bit dated."

"Did you know that diamonds have grades?"

"Well, yes, though I have no idea what that means in practice."

"Take a look at that ring there. See it, the really huge circle-shaped stone. Look at the tag next to it. Can you see that it says G VVS2?"

"Mmmn, but what does that mean?"

"Diamonds are graded. The alphabet denotes

quality. D is the best grade normally available. So E isn't quite as good as D, and G is a lot further down the scale. Above D is museum quality, which you can still get hold of, 'though it takes some doing."

"Really?"

"And the VVS2 refers to the inclusions, the flaws. So VS1 is better than VVS2, fewer flaws."

"So what you're telling me is that that whopper of a stone in the window isn't really very high quality, as compared to what is available? But how can you or I tell?"

"That, Teddi, is why I love you so much. Your intelligence and also your taste."

He was laughing and I must have looked perplexed.

"The multi-hued colours that you dislike so much are actually the flaws. The more visible the flaws, the more multi-hued and disco-glittery the diamond will seem. So what you dislike are the flaws, and what you prefer is the perfect diamond. Such taste."

We'd laughed.

"It's the price that astonishes me, 'though. The price of the ring in that shop window is probably double what it cost the jeweller."

"You know a lot about diamonds, Christoph."

"Done a little research recently. The price of that diamond at a diamond merchant would be a fraction of that cost. Even with the price of the metal, even with platinum, the cost should be half, or even less, of what the jeweller is asking. For that price, if you bypass the jeweller, you could get a D."

"Right. Guess the challenge would be bypassing the jeweller. I mean, I have no idea how you would do that."

"Everything is possible, Teddi. Come on, let's get to the restaurant while we can still get a table." And with that we'd half-run to our favourite café for supper. After which I'd wondered, just wondered, if there had been any other purpose to the conversation than simply idle chatter. I mean, do men regularly research diamonds, even physicists involved in the life changing arena of quantum physics research?

As if that hadn't piqued my curiosity, not long afterwards, over a quiet pre-theatre supper, he'd pulled out his iPad. Now he knows that I am as modern as they come in some ways, but severely old-fashioned in others. Phones, smart or otherwise, laptops, media devices etc., have no place at the dinner table. I detest couples who sit at the table opposite one another merrily poking their chums and ignoring the person sat a metre away from them. Why bother even being there? It isn't even the 'companionable silence' of the long-term married. So pulling out an iPad and firing up Safari whilst at the table had been a bit of a move by Christoph, it had to be said.

"Remember the other day how I said everything is possible? Outside the jewellers? Well I thought I'd check it out, just to see how easy it is. There are diamond merchant in Covent Garden in London will source exactly the diamond you want. You can carry out the entire transaction online. It's amazing. Look at this one, for example."

I'd taken a look. The website he had pulled up was glossy, impeccably laid out. The advertised diamonds looked beautiful, the service exceptional.

"Look, see here they explain all of the diamond grades. And, if you bear with me a moment, you see here they promise to provide full authentication and certification for your diamond."

He was right. The website did indeed offer these services. I made a mental note to wander by the address next week when I was back in London, check whether this was for real. In the end I hadn't gone there, as my trip's whole purpose had been overshadowed somewhat by the political changes globally and back at HQ. It had slipped from my mind.

"What do you think?"

"To be honest, I am amazed. I had no idea this was possible. Though if you think about it, with the advent of the internet, coupled with secure delivery, why not? I'd be nervous though."

"What, about placing an order?"

"Yes, the wait to see if the whole situation is genuine or just a scam. You know me though, I worry too much."

"Yes you do." We'd relaxed, laughing again. Time and again he has told me that I worry too much, that I need to let go of whatever in my childhood has led me into this behavior, and that I should embrace the warmth and depth that others see in me and trust. But it never feels like he is criticizing me, more like I am being gently supported on a personal journey.

"Do you know, they even design jewellry too? Look at this, they have some incredible designs already worked out. They can quote for each design in a variety of metals, for different diamond grades, add engraving, the whole nine yards."

The designs were beautiful, though it seemed hard to picture a ring from the sketches.

"Click on the little hand in the bottom right corner".

And there it was. For each design, a 3D picture of a hand, wearing that ring. That could be rotated through 360 degrees. Short of wearing it yourself, there would be nothing closer to giving you an idea about how it would look on your hand.

I had flicked through designs, messing around with options, and did the same on a couple of other sites.

"Well, I take back any skepticism," I'd said. "These are incredibly invested websites. You know, you can learn more looking at these websites than you ever would in the average jewellers. The designs are beautiful, and you can create a ring to suit the person. It says here they will even create one-off designs. I mean, why doesn't everyone use this sort of service?"

Christoph had smiled.

"But you, Teddi, as ever, have exquisite taste. Take a look at the screen again. Look at the option you've left on the display. Isn't that just you? Elegant and simple, with a D grade stone. Just the right size. Not so big you look like euro-trash, not so small that you blink and miss it."

He was right. It looked lovely.

"Well what can I say?" I'd tried to jest, lightly. "You know me. Think I'd add one nuance though. With diamonds, size isn't everything - I'd rather have a chip of a diamond that was D grade, than a whopper that was H."

"Of course," he'd smiled. "Anyway, I just wanted to show that it can be done, prove I wasn't talking hot air. Now I'll put away the iPad" and he'd smiled again.

"Too right. Next thing you know, we'll be sat opposite one another looking up friends' activity and posting supposed witticisms about the food, whilst ignoring one another. It's a slippery slope."

We had smiled together, a smile of recognition. It's a conversation we've had many times, and agree totally upon. We've decided that life is too short and too precious for social websites. We know friends and colleagues who have fallen out through comments and actions on sites, who decide one another's worth depending upon actions commented upon, regularity and wittiness of postings, and lose ownership of personal information in the process. This before trolls and nastiness.

Truth be told, though, Christoph is also a man's man, and hates the ex-boyfriends who 'get back in touch' to 'reminisce about old times.' I never mention the ex-girlfriends, would-be fuck buddies, frenemies and wannabe stalkers who do the same.

I suspect that Christoph is a man's man and likes to hunt, likes to pursue his girlfriend, likes to think she is desirable, and ultimately worth taking off the market. Why display jealousy over women who mean nothing to him? I mean, if he thought any of them was 'The One' he'd be with her, right? I'd decided that that is how men function.

But with that we had drifted the conversation away from jewellry.

Suddenly, now, though, it all makes sense. Checking out my perspectives on life, and work, and children. Making sure that I stay in Switzerland. Making sure that I love wine-making.

He is standing in front of me, as the sun sets around us, and the sky drifts into a subtle mélange of orange, pink, lilac and purple, talking about serious, 'life,' stuff. I've been so narcissistically self-absorbed that I haven't realized what has been going on. This is it…

"Are you ok, Teddi?"

I nod, looking into his soft, brown eyes. The sounds around us seem to fade into the background, time slows, moves out of focus.

"Teddi," as he kneels before me, and takes my hands in his. "Teddi, will you marry me?"

Oh Christoph, you have no idea. No idea how much I would like to marry you.

I nod. "Yes, Christoph. Yes, I'll marry you."

We're smiling, almost crying. He pulls a small, glossy white box out of his pocket. He opens it. Inside is to most beautiful ring I have ever seen. I know he has had it made just for me. I know it has taken so many romantic steps to get to this place, what he has had to do to turn a dream into reality.

He puts it on my left hand, onto the ring finger. It fits like a glove.

The stone is white. Brilliant white. Icy, deep, breath-taking white.

"Isn't it an amazing stone? D, just like you wanted."

He looks anxious. Perfect, heroic, anxious, so close to his desire.

"Guess now we know why rappers call it 'ice'."

We laugh, gently, into the night. We look at it together, and then at each other. He wraps me into his arms, so tight I can hardly breathe, but I don't notice. Not now.

Dusk is falling around us. We smooch to a silent record, moving perfectly together, drifting into one.

I'm in a country overflowing with millionaires and if I look into the future I have no idea what job I will have. Love, though, is what matters, and I am blessed with love in abundance, I am wealthy indeed.

The End

Acknowledgements

It is with pride and appreciation that I acknowledge those who have contributed to the completion of “The Secret Alchemist.”

Firstly to my daughter and my husband, who have believed in me as a writer and encouraged me to carry on when my own self-doubt threatened to call a halt to the task. Without them this book simply wouldn’t have been completed. You have helped me fufil a lifelong dream.

Thank you also to my husband for supporting me along the way, knowing that writing is what I want to do, and whose tolerance of the long hours involved has been, and is, amazing.

Thank you also for my husband’s lateral thinking and good commonsense in ensuring that I changed the name of the story, and the cover, before publication.

I’ve researched the issues of both executive pay and crowd behaviour in the formation and ‘popping’ of economic bubbles. There are some very accessible reports and books around. I don’t identify any in the story, and no extracts are made therefrom, but my readers can reference those works if they want to see the detail for themselves.

To the inventors of the internet in general, and to e-publishing in particular, I would also like to offer a quiet word of appreciation. Thanks to you, people can follow their dream of becoming a writer.

Finally, a gentle word of thanks to the curators of various writers and writing groups on LinkedIn who have allowed this humble scribe to join their exalted ranks. When I have felt like I would never make it to the end of a chapter, let alone the book, your stories of endeavour and achievement have been a quiet inspiration.

Caroline A Connell
8th April 2013

Please check out my website:
www.carolineaconnell.com

24210307R00152

Printed in Poland
by Amazon Fulfillment
Poland Sp. z o.o., Wrocław